THE
Bronze Pen

Also By
ZILPHA KEATLEY SNYDER

And Condors Danced

Black and Blue Magic

Blair's Nightmare

Cat Running

The Changeling

The Egypt Game

The Famous Stanley
Kidnapping Case

Fool's Gold

The Ghosts of Rathburn Park

Gib and the Gray Ghost

Gib Rides Home

The Gypsy Game

The Headless Cupid

Janie's Private Eyes

Libby on Wednesday

The Magic Nation Thing

The Runaways

Season of Ponies

Song of the Gargoyle

Squeak Saves the Day and Other
Tooley Tales

The Treasures of Weatherby

The Trespassers

The Truth About Stone Hollow

The Unseen

The Velvet Room

The Witches of Worm

THE
Bronze Pen

ZILPHA KEATLEY SNYDER

ATHENEUM BOOKS FOR YOUNG READERS
New York   London   Toronto   Sydney

ATHENEUM BOOKS FOR YOUNG READERS

An imprint of Simon & Schuster Children's Publishing Division

1230 Avenue of the Americas

New York, New York 10020

Book design by Debra Sfetsios

The text for this book is set in Adobe Jenson Pro.

Manufactured in the United States of America

First Edition

10 9 8 7 6 5 4 3 2 1

Library of Congress Cataloging-in-Publication Data

Snyder, Zilpha Keatley.

The bronze pen / Zilpha Keatley Snyder.—1st ed.

p. cm.

Summary: With her father's failing health and the family's shaky finances, twelve-year-old Audrey's dreams of becoming a writer seem very impractical until she is given a peculiar bronze pen that appears to have unusual powers.

ISBN-13: 978-1-4169-4201-6 (hardcover)

ISBN-10: 1-4169-4201-7 (hardcover)

[1. Pens—Fiction. 2. Authorship—Fiction. 3. Magic—Fiction. 4. Family problems—Fiction.] I. Title.

PZ7.S68522Bro 2008

[Fic]—dc22   2006102314

To all furred and feathered messengers

SHE SHOULD HAVE KNOWN BETTER THAN to tell her parents about the woman in the cave. But somehow, sitting at the kitchen table shelling peas while her mother ironed and her father read, Audrey had begun to talk. It hadn't been a conscious decision, but it had suddenly seemed absolutely necessary. And once started, there was no way to stop.

"That cave on Wild Oaks Hill? Way up on that steep hillside, in this weather?" Audrey's mother interrupted before she'd barely begun to explain the situation. "How on earth would an old woman manage to get up there?"

Putting down his newspaper, Audrey's father said, "Do you suppose we ought to do something, Hannah? If the poor thing is homeless, she probably could use some help."

Hannah Abbott, Audrey's mother, came to a quick and firm decision. "Of course. She probably needs to be put in an institution. The police should be notified, and the sooner the better."

"The police?" Audrey and her father asked in unison. And then they went on, talking at once. "No. Not the police," Audrey was saying while her father was asking if that wasn't overdoing it a little. "I shouldn't think it would take a squad of Captain Banner's troopers to bring in one old woman." He was grinning. Audrey's father always grinned when Greendale's chief of police was mentioned. When he had been editor of the *Greendale Times*, he'd gotten to know the spit-and-polish captain only too well. "Just think what a tough decision the captain would have to make," he went on. "He might have to decide whether it was worth getting his shiny boots dirty. Why not notify someone in social services?"

Audrey's mom always used to laugh at her husband's jokes about Old Spit-and-Polish Banner, but this time she didn't even smile. Instead, she said sharply, "And wait two weeks while they complete all the necessary paperwork? I don't think that's a good idea." She was speaking so loudly that Beowulf, the Abbotts' oversized Irish wolfhound, who was sprawled out under the table, raised his head and let out a reproachful bark. Beowulf disapproved of raised voices.

"Well, you do have a point there. Captain Banner it is." Audrey's father was heading toward the telephone when he slowed his wheelchair, his open hand pressed against his chest. "Do you suppose you could make the call, Hannah? I don't feel quite up to dealing with our heroic captain at the moment." Audrey knew what the sarcastic way he said "heroic" meant. But while Captain Banner was easy to joke about, there wasn't anything funny about the pain in John Abbott's chest.

Audrey's mother paused, iron in midair, her famous eyes (Hannah Elgin Abbott had been named the Girl with the Most Beautiful Eyes in her high school yearbook) narrowing with concern. "Yes. Yes, of course, dear," she said. "You go rest until dinner is ready. Don't worry about it. I'll call Captain Banner just as soon as I finish this blouse."

But as soon as her husband disappeared down the hall, Hannah turned back to Audrey. "But first, young lady, I do want to know how you happened to find this woman. You surely remember that when the Mayberry twins were forbidden to go anywhere near that cave, you were too? Of course, you were pretty young at the time, but later, I believe it was after the Mayberrys moved away, you told your father and me that you would never go there again because the cave was—I think the word you used was 'sinister.'"

Hannah Abbott's smile had a softer, reminiscent look to it as she went on. "Yes, I'm sure that was it. I remember your father and I laughed about it being such a grown-up word for a five-year-old to use. Do you remember telling us the cave was a sinister place?"

"I guess so." Audrey shrugged. "It was a long time ago. I might have said that."

She probably had. She'd been using the "sinister" word for a long time. It was an important word for a writer to know—a mysteriously threatening word that was especially useful when you were writing mysteries or scary fantasies. The game in the cave certainly had been awesomely mysterious and scary. She could still remember how excited she'd been when James and Patricia Mayberry let her play, even though they were so much older.

Of course, the most mysterious and sinister part of the game had been the cave itself. But the whole thing—the Mayberry twins' habit of playing the role of evil pirates one day and their terrified, helpless victims the next—had been absolutely thrilling.

But that had all been years ago, and when the Mayberry family moved away, Audrey really had stopped going to the cave. There had been no pirates' cave adventures for Audrey Abbott for at least six or seven years now. Oh, she'd been back briefly once or twice, just to take a quick look around and remember how exciting it had been, but that was all. That was all, that is, until . . .

"I know," she began trying to explain. "I do remember promising not to go there anymore. And I wouldn't have gone back, only I was following a—I mean, I was just following the path, taking a walk up there on the hill, and I happened to glance in the cave. That's all I was doing, just glancing in."

"So you glanced in the cave and you saw this old woman?"

Audrey shook her head. "Not very well," she said. "At the back of the cave it's too dark to see much of anything. But I heard her. She talked to me."

Audrey's mother could narrow her large eyes into lash-fringed slits of suspicion. "How do you suppose she managed to get there? How in the world could an old woman climb all the way up that steep hillside?" Hannah Elgin Abbott's smile changed again, and now there was a familiar edge to it. A suspicious edge that had always meant that, while she wasn't exactly going to say so, she really didn't believe a word that Audrey was saying.

Audrey knew what her mother's smile was implying and why—and suddenly her cheeks were hot and she was clenching her teeth. It was true that when she was younger, she sometimes made up things that didn't really happen and people who didn't really exist, like the friendly ghost who lived in her closet and the baby dragon who liked to hide under her bed. But that had been a long time ago, and the only stories she made up now were the novels she wrote in her secret notebook and never mentioned to anyone, particularly not her mother.

She wanted to argue, to tell her mother how much she resented the implication that even now, when she was twelve years old, she still didn't know the difference between what was real and what wasn't. But it was no time for an argument, not when her parents were about to make such an awful mistake.

In spite of her best effort to cool it, Audrey could feel her voice tightening to an angry squeak as she went on. "Mom, you really don't need to call the police. I mean, I don't think there's anything they can do for—for someone like her. I only told you because I thought you might let me take her something from the garden and maybe a blanket. I don't want you to—"

"Woof!" This time Beowulf's bark was an even sharper reprimand.

"Shh!" Hannah told Beowulf, glancing down the hall toward where her husband was trying to rest.

Audrey felt guilty. She should have known better than to let Beowulf know how angry she was—not when her father might hear the bark and guess that she and her mother were arguing again. Reaching down, she patted Beowulf's huge shaggy head and scratched behind his ears until he sighed and wagged his tail.

"Shh! Good dog," Hannah said, and then to Audrey, "I didn't mean the poor thing should be arrested. It just seems from what you've told us, that she obviously is homeless and probably not able to take care of herself."

Her mother didn't understand. Neither of them did. She should have known they wouldn't. Audrey Abbott should have known she couldn't explain the woman in the cave to her parents. They wouldn't understand even if she started at the very beginning—especially if she started at the absolutely unbelievable beginning—and the white duck.

CHAPTER 2

THE VERY BEGINNING HAD BEEN ONLY A week before, when Audrey had sneaked out of the house to escape some visiting "family friends." Some old friends of her mother's, actually, from way back when her mother and all three of her visitors had been students at Greendale High School. Classmates who nowadays had nothing better to do than sit around asking stupid personal questions, such as, "But, Hannah dear, how have you been able to manage with poor John so ill for such a long time?"

One of the women, the one named Maribel, had asked that very question when "poor John," Audrey's father, had just wheeled himself out of the room and still might have been within earshot. Remembering the simpering, phony sympathy in the woman's voice, Audrey couldn't help cringing—and biting her lip in anger.

According to Audrey's mother, the visitors were "well-meaning," but there were other ways to look at it. The way Audrey saw it, the way anyone would who'd looked through those old Greendale High School yearbooks, was that at least a couple of the visitors had come to gloat more than to sympathize. To gloat because back in their high school days they probably had been jealous of Hannah Elgin, whose glamorous senior picture had been labeled the Girl with the Most Beautiful Eyes, and who had been elected Homecoming queen two years in a row. While the "well-meaning" visitors . . . Well, Audrey had seen their pictures too—not that they were that much to look at.

But when Hannah Elgin Abbott's husband had become an invalid and the old Elgin house, which had once been one of the nicest in town, was . . . Audrey had seen them sneaking sideways glances at the old-fashioned TV, the saggy couch, and, in one corner of the living room, the dirty old baby crib mattress that was Beowulf's sleeping pad—not to mention a few badly scarred chair legs, which he'd cut his teeth on when he was an enormous puppy.

That was it, all right. Audrey was certain of it. Not that she was a mind reader, but you didn't have to be psychic to know what those snooty women were up to, in their expensive outfits with shoes that matched the color of their dresses. Bright green shoes to go with a green polka dot dress, believe it or not.

So Audrey had escaped while the three visitors were still sitting in the Abbotts' living room talking to Audrey's mother and perhaps to her father again, if he had begun to feel a little better. While Audrey, herself, was in one of her favorite writing hideouts, sitting cross-legged on a slightly damp patch of grass on the highest terrace behind the house, with her secret notebook and a nicely sharpened pencil, trying to get over being angry by putting her mind on her latest story.

As usual, it began to work almost at once. After only a few minutes she calmed down enough to really get into it. That was one of the great things about being an author, even a secret one. It was usually possible to get your head so full of the people you were writing about that you could, at least temporarily, block out all kinds of other stuff—and people.

She was just getting into the second chapter of a story called "Heather's Alley Adventure," in which a girl detective who can talk to animals was about to solve a terrible murder by talking to a witness to the crime, who happened to be a cat. At least the cat claimed to be a witness, only it was going to turn out that it was lying. And instead of helping Heather, it was actually trying to lure her to a dark alley where the killer was lying in wait.

She thought she had done a good job on the scary foreshadowing—describing the cat's evil yellow eyes and the mysterious shapes and sounds in the dark alley. She had just written:

"Meow, meow," the cat said, but what Heather's supernatural ears heard was,

"Follow me, my dear, and I will lead you to an important clue."

The alley didn't look at all inviting but because she hadn't yet deduced that the cat was a traitor, Heather listened to what it had to say. Pushing her flowing blond hair out of her beautiful blue eyes, Heather followed the cat.

The story was going so well that re-reading what she had just written had made the hair on the back of Audrey's neck start to quiver when she suddenly became aware of a sound that definitely had not been a product of her imagination. Something was moving through the bushes behind her back. Something real and solid. Dropping her notebook, Audrey jumped up, whirled around—and there it was. A large white duck was standing only a few feet away.

Even that first time, when the duck appeared so suddenly, Audrey wasn't terribly surprised. It was almost as if she had been expecting it. She hadn't, of course, but if the duck had seemed slightly familiar, she could think of a possible reason. One that went back to when her grandmother, Nellie Elgin, used to tell stories about a wonderful duck she had known when she was a little girl. A white duck named Lily who was her special friend and who had lived on the farm where she grew up. Grandma Nellie talked about ducks a lot, and because of having known an intelligent duck like Lily, Grandma Nellie, who quite often fried chickens, refused to cook or eat ducks.

And now a white duck had suddenly appeared right there on the high terrace. A visitor who, while it did seem to be watchful and alert, didn't appear to be the least bit afraid. The word "tame" crossed Audrey's mind and then was quickly erased. Where this calm, dignified creature was concerned, the word "tame" somehow seemed like an insult.

Calmly turning its sleek oval head one way and then the other, the duck continued to eye Audrey as she sank down to her knees, held out an upturned hand, and whispered, "Hello, duck." It nodded then, acknowledging her greeting, and after turning its head to inspect her with one eye and then the other, it waddled closer and bent its neck until its beak lay in Audrey's outstretched palm. A wide, yellow beak, as smoothly solid as a wooden ruler, and yet somehow warm and alive. For two or three seconds the duck's bill remained in her hand before it pulled away, turned, and disappeared into the surrounding underbrush.

Audrey jumped to her feet and pushed her way into the bushes, peering from side to side and calling out, "Here, duck. Come back, duck. Where did you go?" But it was useless. It had disappeared.

So that Saturday was the first meeting, but not the last. The very next day in the early afternoon Audrey once again visited the high terrace, this time bringing with her some bread crumbs and, in a paper cup, a few spoonfuls of Sputnik's birdseed.

Once again she sat down exactly where she had been the day before and settled herself to wait—but not for long. She had only enough time to unwrap the bread and seeds and spread them out on a page torn from her notebook when suddenly it was there again. Once again inspecting Audrey with one eye and then the other, it moved forward and eagerly helped itself to the bread and seeds. And when the last bit of food had disappeared, it moved even closer and, once again, reached out to touch her hand with its bill.

After that brief moment of contact the duck raised its head, started away, and stopped to look back with a sharp nod that left Audrey absolutely certain that she was supposed to follow—and she did. To follow a duck who, like Lily in her grandmother's stories, knew how to lead people to places they should go. In Lily's case it had often been to where a person could make herself useful by turning over a stone or brick to uncover a tasty bunch of worms and sow bugs.

"All right. I'm coming," Audrey said. "I'm following you. Where are the worms?" And she did follow, only a few steps behind, as the duck waddled with awkward dignity across the high terrace and through the grove of saplings on the far edge of her family's property—and kept on going. Kept going past several rocky places where there might be good worm hunting and continued on, even when Audrey tried to tempt it by turning over a flat rock and a chunk of tree bark.

The duck's shuffling gait was not swift, but it seemed to cover ground with surprising efficiency. Skirting trees and bushes, on paths that were still damp from the recent rain, it paused to look back now and then before continuing on up the slope that led toward the foothills. Paused, and then, when Audrey was lagging too far behind, flapped its wings and nodded its head in a way that clearly meant for her to hurry. No longer bothering to detour around the muddiest places, Audrey made an effort to keep up, but as she slid and skidded on the narrow path, she thought, more than once, that the duck seemed not only confident, but also strangely demanding for a common barnyard fowl. A barnyard fowl, but on the other hand, perhaps something much more.

They'd crossed the first shallow gully and started up the next steep rise before Audrey began to guess where they were going. Guessed, and then wondered why. Why would a duck be going to such a place? Ducks, as far as she knew, were not cave dwellers.

But her guess proved to be a good one. The duck continued to follow the secret trail that Audrey remembered very well from the days of the Mayberry pirates. It wasn't long before it reached the bottom of an almost vertical cliff, and the entrance to the forbidden cave.

CHAPTER 3

JUST AS SHE REMEMBERED, THE HILLSIDE was almost covered by a thick growth of ivy that cascaded down the slope in long leafy coils. She remembered the ivy, but there was much more of it now, so thickly overgrown that the entrance to the cave was almost hidden. Audrey stopped and watched as the duck headed directly toward a narrow opening in the heavy curtain of vine. It stopped one more time to look back before disappearing.

After pausing doubtfully for only a second, Audrey was about to follow when she was startled by a flurry of sound and motion, as if the whole hill had suddenly come to life. All across the hillside green leaves quivered and shook as dozens of small dark birds erupted from the ivy, chirping frantically.

Audrey staggered back, throwing up her hands to protect her head as the blackbirds surrounded her, their fluttering wings brushing her face and hair before they took off to disappear into a nearby grove of trees. Blackbirds living in the ivy? She didn't remember them. No birds when she was there before, not even one. She was quite certain of that.

She was still staring, first at the now limp and silent vines and then off toward the trees, when the duck reappeared. But only briefly, to nod at her impatiently, before it disappeared back through the ivy curtain. A flicker of memory reminded Audrey of something she had just written. The part about how Heather had risked her life by following an animal into a dark alley. And then she was allowing herself to be led into a secret and sinister cave.

Once inside, it was surprisingly dark. Much darker than she remembered from when she was there with the Mayberrys. But the entrance had been more open then, less covered by the curtain of vine.

It took a long moment for Audrey's eyes to adjust to the semidarkness. But the smell was immediately familiar—a heavy, earthy odor that hinted at things that oozed or slithered. Then the shadows gradually receded, and near the front of the cave dim shapes began to materialize. Her first impression was that nothing had changed. On each side rough rocky walls arched up over an area as large as a long narrow room. An almost empty room, except where two sawhorses supported some long splintery planks surrounded by apple crates—an arrangement that had served as a table and chairs in the days of the Mayberrys' game. Other than the remains of pirate furniture, there had been only a messy pile of old rugs and blankets stacked up against the rear wall, but now that whole area was lost in darkness.

Nothing much to see, but now Audrey was becoming aware of noises. From the darkness at the back of the cave came some soft clacking, hissing sounds and, from farther up, a series of tiny squeaks. She took another step into the darkness, and now, far up on the wall, a row of white faces were looking down at her. White faces with huge round eyes and sharp pointed beaks.

Gasping, she was backing away when her fright changed into surprised recognition—owls, barn owls. Along with ducks, Grandma Nellie had been particularly fond of barn owls. Audrey came to a stop and started back. The owls' round eyes gazed unblinkingly and their white faces quivered as they emitted another chorus of hoots and hisses.

But there were still those other sounds. A dim whispery chorus of squeaks and squeals that seemed to be coming from . . . Audrey listened and then, following the sound, looked up to where a large patch of the cave's rocky ceiling seemed to have come to life. Staring down at her were dozens, maybe hundreds, of large round eyes in pointed foxy faces. The ceiling of the cave was alive with bats.

Grandma Nellie had known a lot, not only about owls, but also about bats. So Audrey knew, at least her mind knew, that bats were harmless, useful creatures, but another part of her wasn't so sure. There were, it seemed, hidden feelings that came from rumors that bats would suck your blood—or at least tangle themselves in your hair. She was backing away, her hands protecting her head, when there was a new sound. This time a loud squawking noise that came from the back of the cave.

In the silent gloom of the cave the noise was startlingly loud, almost frightening. "Ack," it said. "Ack, ack, ack." The harsh sound was all she heard. Not exactly a quack—as Audrey looked quickly from side to side, she saw there was no sign of the duck; it seemed to have disappeared. But whatever the noise was, it seemed to quiet all the others.

As Audrey turned back toward the darkness at the end of the cave, she began to be aware of motion. Something was moving back there. As if coming out of nowhere, an indistinct figure seemed to be materializing—a dim, unrecognizable something . . . or someone. As Audrey blinked hard and went on staring, she gradually began to sense, if not quite see, a strangely shapeless figure, draped in a long dark cape, who seemed to be sitting or crouching against the far wall. It wasn't until it spoke that Audrey was entirely sure it was alive—and human.

"Well, well," a creaky voice said. "Welcome to my private abode, my dear." And then, before Audrey could even begin to imagine answering, it went on. "I thank you for coming."

Audrey swallowed hard and managed to say, "Are you—are you talking to me?"

It wasn't until then, when the thing at the back of the cave shook its head and emitted a high cackling laugh, that Audrey began to think of it as female. "Yes, I am, my dear," the weird, high-pitched, squawky voice went on. "And I am looking forward to conversing with you. I know we have much in common, or you wouldn't be here. I imagine we will have some important things to say to each other. Don't you agree?"

"Well, I—I guess so," Audrey was stammering when the creature—the woman, whatever it was—continued.

"For instance, you could begin by telling me about yourself. About what you have become."

"About myself? You mean my name and—"

"No, no. Never mind that," the voice said impatiently. "Names aren't important. *What* is much more important. That is something I would very much like to know. *What* you are doing, for instance, and *what* is important to you."

Audrey was at a loss. She didn't understand what was being asked of her any more than she understood what— or who—it was that was asking. She still seemed unable to see more than the faintest shadow of whatever it was at the back of the cave. The deep shadow was part of the problem, but there was more to it than that. The dim figure seemed to be constantly changing, in size and shape.

"What do I do?" she asked. Was that a nod? It seemed to be, so she blundered on. "I just go to school. I'm only twelve years old."

"Ah. I see. But what do you plan to do, forever and always? With all your days and years?"

What did she plan to do with all her days and years? Audrey suppressed a critical smirk. It was such a weird way to put the question. A question that she knew the answer to, of course, not that she would share it with anyone. Particularly not with a creepy old creature who seemed to be something out of a strangely vivid dream.

She was assuring herself that she would never think of telling this woman what her plan for the future was when suddenly she heard a voice speaking—her own voice. With her eyes cast down toward the cave's muddy floor, she suddenly heard herself say, "I want to be an author. I want to write stories."

She stopped abruptly then, not only amazed and shocked by what she had already said, but frightened, too. Afraid of the strange creature who seemed to be able not only to read her mind, but also to force her to say things she definitely hadn't meant to say.

"Ah, yes." The creature's head seemed to be bobbing up and down in a strangely birdlike way. "Ah, yes, I see."

Along with shaken surprise, there was now anger as well. What right did this person—did anyone—have to force her to talk about her private plans? And she had been forced. She had no idea how it had been done, but she knew it had. Otherwise, she would never have mentioned a secret she'd never told anyone—not even her closest friends.

Shoulders squared against a surge of fear mixed with anger, Audrey backed away. She would just turn around now and leave. Yes. That's what she would do. She was at the mouth of the cave, reaching up to push aside the curtain of vine, when the creaky voice called after her. "Come back, child. You must come back."

Audrey paused long enough to say, "No. I'm going. I have to go now and I'm not going to—that is, I don't think I can—come back." She meant it when she said it, but even as the words left her mouth, she knew that they might not be true. And she somehow felt certain that the woman knew they weren't.

As she made her way back down the Mayberry pirates' hidden path, what she had said about never coming back was only part of a larger uncertainty about everything that had just happened and what might only have seemed to be happening. Of what might be only a particularly vivid product of her "overactive imagination."

The duck had been real, she was sure of that. There was no way she could have imagined that solid, sturdy whiteness and the confidence of that black-eyed stare. It was possible to imagine that someone could be tempted into danger by the slit yellow eyes of a cat. But to sense such evil purpose in the shiny black eyes of a duck? That seemed, somehow, impossible.

And the rest of it? The creature—old woman—whatever—in the pirates' cave. That hooded shape with its birdlike cackle. How much of it had been the product of her imagination? Of that overactive imagination that, as she had so often been told, was sometimes way out of control? As Audrey made her way down the steep, slippery path, there were still so many questions without answers.

CHAPTER 4

IT WASN'T AFTER THAT FIRST VISIT THAT Audrey told her parents about the woman in the cave. She thought about telling them, of course, but for more reasons than one, she decided against it. In the first place there was the fact that she had been forbidden to go there. Had, in fact, promised never to visit the cave again. That, by itself, was a good enough reason not to have mentioned it. But there was more to it than that.

The other reason was a lot harder to put her finger on, but it had something to do with the possibility that some of it had been added to, at least a little bit, by her imagination. That sort of thing, Audrey had to admit, had happened before. There was, for instance, the time when she had gone with her mother to put flowers on her grandparents' graves and she'd heard a voice reminding her to water her grandmother's favorite rosebush. She'd been sure, or almost sure, of what she'd heard, and she'd told her mother so. But after a while she herself began to wonder whether it had been a real voice or only, as her mother insisted that day in the graveyard, a well-remembered one.

And now, on the evening of that first visit to the cave, Audrey was still sorting it out. Trying to narrow it down to the things she was absolutely certain of, while at the same time cleaning the cockatiel's cage and half listening to what her mother was saying about yesterday's visitors. It wasn't easy.

For one thing Sputnik, the cockatiel, was, or at least tried to be, a dangerous bird. John, Audrey's dad, had rescued him from a reporter at the *Greendale Times*, who had called him Bleep and had threatened to throw him to the chicken hawks because he was hopelessly mean and foulmouthed.

Andy Anderson, the reporter, had been right about the foulmouthed part. Sputnik certainly did know how to swear. The Abbotts had changed his name from Bleep to Sputnik not because he'd stopped swearing, but because of his tendency to go into orbit whenever he escaped from his cage. So cleaning Sputnik's cage was never easy, but Audrey had discovered she could do it without being pecked or sworn at if she ignored his threats and moved quickly and quietly.

"They do mean well," Hannah was still insisting. "At least Virginia does." Adding freshly peeled carrots to the stew pot, Hannah Abbott turned and gave Audrey a rueful smile. "I do have to admit that Maribel always did have a mean streak. I remember one time in Mr. Martin's chemistry class . . ."

It was about then that Audrey lost track completely of what her mother was saying as she focused once more on what she had seen in the cave.

There had been the duck and then the slippery trip up the muddy path. Of that much, she was absolutely certain. But then there was the cave itself and the strange creature—an old woman, perhaps. Audrey closed her eyes and tried to picture exactly what she had seen. Some of it wasn't hard to recall.

The vine-covered entrance to the cave and the rickety table and chairs were all as clear as if a negative had been imprinted on the inside of her eyelids. And the owls and bats as well were easy to picture. But farther back, almost hidden in the deepest shadows, there was only movement and a vague, ever-changing shape and the sound of a raspy, high-pitched voice. A remembered sound that was now competing with Sputnik's squawks.

But in spite of having to cope with a bad-tempered cockatiel, Audrey was still managing to concentrate pretty well on what had happened in the cave until her visual memories were interrupted by something even more distracting. Something cold and wet was pressing on the back of her right leg.

Beowulf's arrivals were usually announced by pants and snuffles and clicking toenails, but this time, because of Sputnik's uproar, Audrey had heard nothing before his nose made contact with her bare skin. Dropping to her knees, she wrapped her arms around the big shaggy head and shook it.

"You sneaky thing. You scared me," she told him, glad for his familiar, comforting warmth. They were still wrestling on the floor with her arms wrapped around his neck and most of her left hand inside his big gentle mouth when the wheelchair's whiny rattle announced her father's arrival.

"Hey, Wulfy, knock it off," John Abbott was saying. "A guy who's supposed to avoid excitement shouldn't have to watch a member of his family being eaten alive."

Audrey giggled, and Beowulf's growling gurgle seemed to mean he got the joke. He went on growling—doing his killer-dog bit—while Audrey pulled her hand out of his mouth, wiped it on his head, and went to hug her father.

Hannah Abbott was almost smiling too as she said, "And now that you're through being eaten alive, please don't forget to wash your hands before you set the table."

"Good idea, kiddo," John told Audrey. "You and I might not mind having Irish wolfhound slobber on our first course, but in today's world we might be in the minority."

Beowulf's slobber was another subject the Abbotts often joked about, but this time it was a different part of what her father said that stuck in Audrey's mind. It was the part about "in today's world" that came and went and came again as she set the table and even after she sat down to eat.

"In today's world." It was a phrase that Audrey's father often used when he talked with her about all sorts of things. Important things that were going on all over the world and that were written about in newspapers and magazines. Particularly in the *Greendale Times* where John Abbott was—or had been—the editor.

But at the moment "today's world" meant the world as it existed in the spring of 1973, in the state of California, in the town of Greendale. A world that, on this particular day, was a place where a person's father could have something called "angina pectoris," which meant that he had to spend most of his time in bed. And where that same person's little, skinny mother had to go back to work at a job she hated, besides doing most of the work in a big old house and in what had once been a prizewinning vegetable garden.

Glancing at her mother, whose thin face made her famous eyes look even larger, Audrey suppressed a sigh and slid into a familiar guilt thing about not doing enough to help around the house. But feeling guilty did have an escape route she'd used many times before, by way of a favorite daydream. The dream about how, after her first published book became a famous bestseller, she would build a mansion for her folks to live in and hire servants to do all the work. And she would find the best doctors in the whole world, who would have discovered a wonderful cure for angina pectoris. And then, in that "world of today," everything would be as good as, or even better than, it used to be.

The famous-author daydream kept reappearing all through dinner and even came back in bits and pieces while Audrey was helping clear the table and clean up the kitchen. A dream that included being recognized and admired wherever she went and having to sign thousands of autographs. But once she was alone again, in her own room, it quickly faded into a different scene. One that was more immediate and demanding and at least a little bit more real. A scene that took place in a forbidden cave and included a strange, half-seen creature and a white duck.

Lying in her bed late that night, still wide awake and still trying to think it all through, Audrey gradually came to a decision. It was beginning to seem more and more important for her to go back just once more. To go back if only to be absolutely sure how much of it had been the way she remembered it and not simply another case of "overactive imagination."

CHAPTER 5

SHE DID GO BACK, OF COURSE, BUT NOT right away since Monday was the beginning of another school week. A week in which Audrey, as always, had to hurry home so her father wouldn't have to be alone any longer than absolutely necessary. It would be best, according to Dr. Richards, if someone could be there constantly to call for an ambulance if John were to suddenly become unconscious. But with Hannah working and Audrey in school, and with no money to pay for a daytime nurse, that wasn't possible. So Hannah worked the late shift at her office, and by taking an early class and skipping study hall, Audrey was able to get home by one o'clock. That left only about two hours in the middle of the day when John Abbott had to be alone.

On Tuesday the weather was warm and dry, and on her way home on the city bus Audrey looked out toward the hills and pictured herself scrambling up the trail that led to the cave. It just might be possible today to get away for a little while when her father was busy reading. She had begun to imagine what it would be like and what she might see when a different scene began to take over. The same one that had so often oozed out of the dark corners of her mind in the long months since her father's heart attack. A homecoming scene in which she ran into the house calling out, *Dad. Dad, I'm home.* And there was no answer.

So every day all that week, just like every week, from early afternoon until her mother got home at almost seven, Audrey was with her father, reading to him or listening to him read, playing chess or checkers, or simply doing her homework while he read the paper. For a while there had been some TV watching. Not much, because they both preferred reading, but none at all lately because the ancient TV wasn't working well, and all the new ones were too expensive.

It was still early on Friday afternoon when, on her way to the kitchen to make some tea, Audrey stopped in a spot of sunshine that was spilling in through the dining room window. Paused long enough to stare up toward the distant hillside, trying to follow the trail with her eyes and once again letting her mind wander back to the strange things that had happened last weekend. Back to the strangely demanding duck and the old woman who could not only read minds, but somehow knew how to make people reveal their deepest secrets.

She was still looking out the window when she heard her father say her name. Just, "Audrey?" but with a questioning rise at the end, and when she turned to look at him, his smile and raised eyebrow did ask a question before his expression faded into something that looked like an apology.

And then John Abbott said it out loud. "I'm so sorry about you having to be cooped up in here with me every afternoon. I'll bet you could find a lot of exciting things to do if you didn't have to rush home to babysit your old man. Things like you and Debra used to do, for instance."

Audrey smiled and shrugged. "It's okay," she said. "I don't mind." But she did mind, at least she did right at that moment, because of the need to get away, and her father probably knew it. He was pretty good at knowing what a person meant, even when they didn't quite say it. But she did go on to add, "And as far as Debra goes, that was over a long time ago."

"I've wondered about that," her father said. "Just kind of outgrew each other, I guess?"

"Yeah," Audrey said. "Something like that."

Having Debra as a best friend had begun soon after the Feltons moved into the old Mayberry house, just three houses down from the Abbotts, and Audrey had discovered that one of their kids was a girl who was just her age.

At the time Audrey had thought the fact that Debra's

family had moved into the Mayberry house was a good omen. As if the old brown-shingled house was somehow destined to provide her with special friends—and she went on thinking so for quite a while. It wasn't long before she and Debra were sitting next to each other every day on the school bus and then spending at least an hour or two together after school, either at the Abbotts' or the Feltons'. More often at the Abbotts', actually, after Debra's older siblings started spying on them and making fun of their games. Games like making fairy circles in the acacia grove and mixing magic potions, which, when secretly applied to people's hands and foreheads—people like Debra's big brother—were supposed to make them into enlightened people. Or at least a little easier to get along with.

In those days Debra had really liked their games. Not that she was good at thinking them up, but she was always very enthusiastic about Audrey's ideas. And when she told Audrey she had a big imagination, she usually, but not always, said it in a complimentary way.

But then things had begun to change. Even before Audrey's father got sick and she had to be at home every afternoon, Debra had started being less interested in the kinds of things she and Audrey had done. Little by little they'd pretty much stopped spending time together, even when they had a chance.

"Debra's too busy trying to be a hippie, I guess," Audrey told her father now, and then, wanting to change the subject, she added, "Let's talk about something else. Something more interesting."

"All right. I vote for that," her father said. "Let's see!" He turned his chair in a circle, looking around the room. "Something to make things a little more exciting? I know. We could let Sputnik out if you think you could round him up before your mother gets home. That's sure to liven things up a bit."

It was a good idea, but a quick roundup plan would be necessary. Although Hannah Abbott claimed to be a bird lover like her mother, she had very little patience with pint-size parrot types who nibbled chunks out of the woodwork and pooped on the dining room table. At least not when she had just returned from work, tired and, more often than not, a little bit cranky.

Audrey headed for the cockatiel's cage, saying, "Oh, I can catch him, all right." And to Sputnik himself, "If you won't go in when I tell you to I'll just have to get the butterfly net. Won't I?"

As his door opened, Sputnik shrieked a rude answer and, as always, went into orbit. Around the room he flew, squawking madly, shrieking as he hung upside down from the chandelier, then flying again and dipping down to barely miss their faces—Audrey's, John's, even Beowulf's. It wasn't until he'd threatened to land on each of their heads several times that he settled for Beowulf's, where he proceeded to strut up and down, dragging his wing tips and whistling a tuneless, wordless something that managed to sound like a challenge.

For a while Beowulf, a natural-born pacifist, only sighed, grunted, closed his eyes, and pretended to go back to sleep. But Sputnik went on being typically aggressive, pecking Beowulf's ears and screaming four-letter words, until the dog threw him off by shaking his head. After several attacks Beowulf's patience wore out, and he began to growl and show his teeth every time his tormentor got anywhere near him.

This time the big dog's snarls were more convincingly ferocious than usual, and Audrey began to worry that he might really lose it. One bite from Beowulf and no more Sputnik, that was for sure. But when she asked her father if he thought that was a possibility, he only grinned.

"Don't worry," he said. "He'd probably spit him out. Anything as mean as that crazy bird is sure to taste awful."

The dog-and-bird show did make the time pass quickly, and it was getting dangerously close to seven o'clock when Audrey finally had to convince Sputnik to go home by threatening him with the butterfly net. Still squawking four-letter words, he swooped back into his cage just as Hannah's car came down the driveway.

It was a close call. It wouldn't have done for Sputnik to be on the loose when Hannah got home that particular day, because it had been an especially bad one. According to Hannah, Mrs. Austin, her boss at the savings and loan, had been even meaner and more unreasonable than usual, which resulted in a worse-than-usual headache.

So a typical week came to an end, and then it was Saturday. With Hannah at home to look after John, it might have been possible to sneak up to the cave—if it hadn't been for the rain. The rain went on and on, but in the late afternoon Audrey went so far as to put on her mother's gardening boots and an old raincoat and start out up the path. However, she had gone only a few steps before she turned back, realizing there was no way she could make it all the way up the steep, rain-slick trail.

But Sunday morning was clear and warmer, and right after breakfast Audrey began to plan her getaway to the cave. Actually, it shouldn't be too difficult. On Saturdays and Sundays, Audrey often spent time alone either in her room or on one of the terraces when the weather was good. Time spent supposedly reading or doing homework, but more often working on her latest novel. So neither of her parents would worry if she disappeared for a while. But just to make sure, she was careful to set the stage.

Not long after lunch was over, she made it a point to spend a few minutes at the living room's bookshelves near where her father was reading while her mother did a crossword puzzle. After very obviously going over every bookshelf, she carefully chose *Jane Eyre* and *Great Expectations*, books she'd already read at least once, in case her parents should, as they often did, want to discuss what she'd been reading. With the books held conspicuously under her arm, she crossed the room, took off down the hall toward her bedroom, turned back, and tiptoed toward the back of the house.

Out on the back porch she stashed the books on a shelf above the washing machine, between a box of detergent and a bottle of bleach, before starting up the brick steps that led to the highest terrace. Arriving there a little out of breath, she turned slowly in a circle, looking and listening. It was the same place where she'd been before, but now there was nothing to see but grass and stiff, silent bushes. She sat down and waited for quite a long time, but the silence continued. There was no movement among the leaves and no sound at all.

This meant she would have to make the decision all by herself: Should she go on to the cave or simply go back home? She hadn't come to any conclusion, at least not one she remembered making, but suddenly she was on her way, scrambling up the steep, slippery path that led across barren stretches of hillside and through groves of trees until, tired and breathless, she came to a stop at the vine-hung entrance to the cave.

No flight of blackbirds this time. Not even after she stepped closer and waved her arms. But there was something. A soft murmur of birdlike chatter and, as she moved nearer, the slightest shiver of motion among the green leaves. As if the birds were there, hiding in the ivy but not bothering to fly away.

She was stepping closer, raising a hand to move a strand of vine, when suddenly she heard it. A series of strange noises were coming from inside the cave. Noises that didn't contain actual words but, at the same time, managed to sound a lot like an argument. A mixture of squeaks and rasps and squawks that certainly seemed to be saying something accusatory and argumentative. She paused, her mind wavering between concern and curiosity. Curiosity won. Pushing aside the curtain of vine, Audrey went in.

For a moment, just as before, her eyes were almost useless in the dim light, but her ears were working fine, and what they heard was a hushed moment of silence, followed by an avalanche of other sounds. An angry chorus of rasps and squeaks and squeals that for a moment seemed to come out of nowhere and everywhere. Once again Audrey began to see several pairs of round eyes in heart-shaped white faces, staring at her from a high ledge.

And then a creaky voice was saying, "Well, well. So you have come back to see us. I'm so glad."

And there it was. Sitting, just as before, on the bundle of rugs and blankets was the caped and cloaked figure. Except that now Audrey could see a bit more clearly. Could see a pale oval that might be a face and a pair of round, unblinking black eyes.

As the noise level in the cave continued to rise, the

strange creature's face tipped upward and her voice became louder and more demanding. "All right, you rascals. All of you. Stop this nonsense. Be silent." And suddenly it was.

"There! You see?" the creaky voice said. "There's no reason for such a fuss. And you're upsetting our guest." And then to Audrey, "They know quite well they're not allowed to engage in any deviltry in my presence, yet they feel compelled to complain about one another. But they will compose themselves now."

Audrey looked up to see the owls' round faces stop bobbing and quivering, and then farther up where the blanket of bats had become still and silent.

"So, my dear," the woman said, gesturing toward the pirate furniture. "Do sit and we can have our little chat."

CHAPTER 6

N O." AUDREY SHOOK HER HEAD. SHE hadn't come to chat. "I only came because . . ." She paused. She couldn't very well say that she'd come to be sure of what she'd seen, or thought she'd seen, before. "But I could sit for a minute," she said instead. Pulling up one of the boxes, she sat down. "But I'm not going to—" She stopped. Or something stopped her.

Taking a deep, shaky breath, she started again, but this time what she said was, "The doctor thinks my father is dying. He had a heart attack almost two years ago and now he has something called angina pectoris. It hurts him a lot, and the doctor wants him just to stay in bed all the time, but he gets up and sits in a chair sometimes. A wheelchair. But he can't work anymore. He used to be the editor of the newspaper and he taught journalism at Greendale College, but now he just . . . sits there."

Almost without taking another breath, she went on.

"We live in this house my grandparents built, and my grandmother lived with us until she died. She always won prizes at the fair for the stuff she grew in her garden. My grandmother loved flowers and birds, especially ducks."

"Especially ducks?" The creaky voice had another ripple to it. Almost like a giggle.

"Yes, especially ducks," Audrey said slowly, thinking it was odd she hadn't thought of that strange coincidence before. "Well, one duck, anyway. A white duck who lived on the farm where my grandmother grew up. The duck was named Lily, and my grandma said it was as smart as most dogs, or even smarter, and whenever it saw my grandmother, it would try to lead her to a place where she could help it look for things it wanted to eat."

Audrey stopped talking, gasped, and shook her head hard. What was she doing? Just what she'd promised herself she would never do. The gasp had hardly died away when her voice began again: "And my mother used to be famous too, for being beautiful. And she used to paint and write poetry and take care of our house and garden, but now she has to work in a place where she just keeps track of other people's money, and she has a mean boss and the work is hard and boring, and when she comes home she's too . . ." Her voice trailed away, and, just as before, as soon as she stopped, she felt mostly amazed, but angry, too. Mostly at herself, for doing just what she'd promised herself she wouldn't do, but also furious at the weird creature who was somehow making her do it.

Audrey clamped her lips shut, raised her head, and stared right into the pale, round-eyed face, trying to make her own eyes say that she wasn't going to say anymore. Not a word more.

But the creature asked another question. This time it was only, "And you, my dear?"

And somehow Audrey was saying, at least a voice that seemed to come from some deep part of her was saying, "And I have to come home early from school every afternoon to be with my father, and . . . and I don't mind at all—at least I don't most of the time. But I can't see my friends, except at school, or go anywhere with them, and my friend Debra spends all her time with other people now and doesn't even phone me anymore and . . ."

She wanted to stop. She desperately wanted to, but she might not have, even then, except now the strange creature was talking again, and this time it was saying, "I see. Yes, yes. I see. I do understand."

"No, you don't," Audrey said angrily, but along with the anger, there was another sensation that felt almost like relief. Like the way you feel when something you had to do, but didn't want to do, was finally over and done with. "But telling you all of that—all of that stuff— isn't why I came here. I only came because I wondered if . . . That is, I've been wondering if I could bring you something." It really was a small part of what she'd been planning, but as soon as she said it, she knew it was true and that she meant what she said.

"Something?" The hooded head tipped to one side questioningly.

"Yes. Something to eat, maybe. Something from our garden. I mean, do you have enough to eat?" She glanced around, at the bare table and empty boxes, then at the caped and shapeless figure who still seemed to hover at the edge of darkness. "Or else maybe a blanket or something?"

The hooded head nodded slowly as the rusty voice said, "Don't concern yourself, my dear. I have everything I need. But it was good of you to want to help." The creature was leaning forward now, the white face becoming almost visible, almost familiar, certainly womanlike. "So good of you, my dear."

Audrey backed away, feeling uneasy about what she might be going to say next. "I think I'd better go now." She glanced at her watch. "Yes. I have to go. It's late."

Still nodding, the woman said, "Yes. Perhaps you should go, but wait a moment." The nodding stopped, then began again. "Yes, yes. I know now. Just the right thing."

Turning to one side, she seemed to be searching for something either in the pile of rags she was sitting on or perhaps in a pocket of her long, flowing cloak. The searching went on for several seconds before she said, "Aha! Here, my dear. This is for you."

The old woman's hand, or something a little bit like a

hand, was reaching out again, and Audrey's hand slowly and uncertainly moved toward it until her fingers touched, not fingers, but a feathery softness and, in its midst, a hard round object. And then there in the center of Audrey's palm was a small metal rod that came to a point on one end like a . . . Yes, it was a pen. An old, perhaps ancient, pen made out of a dark, almost rust-colored metal and covered with strange marks and scratches. Except that ancient pens weren't ballpoints, and this one seemed to have that kind of tip.

Audrey was still examining the pen as the quavery voice began saying something unintelligible. A chantlike flow of syllables that rose and fell and rose again, then became louder and more clear. "For you, my dear. Use it wisely and to good purpose." The hooded head seemed to be nodding now as it faded away into the deeper shadow. "But I do think you must go now. Go back to your people. And remember—wisely and to good purpose."

At that moment several things began to happen. A rasping hiss drifted down from the ledge at the back of the cave, immediately followed by a mutter of soft squeaks. The white faces of the owls were bobbing up and down again, and overhead the blanket of bats was once again astir. The noises grew in volume until a harsh, scolding squawk, almost a quack, cut them off. In the silence that followed, Audrey headed toward the light.

She had passed the pirates' saggy table and one of the

makeshift chairs, and was reaching out to push aside the veil of vine when the squawking, quacking sound came again. But closer now, and not so harsh and demanding. Suddenly there it was. From just outside the cave entrance, the white duck was staring at Audrey, first with one black eye and then the other. She whispered, "Good-bye." Turning it into a question, she repeated, "Good-bye, duck?" The duck's sleek oval head bobbed up and down as if in reply before it turned away and disappeared behind the curtain of vine. And then Audrey was on her way down the hill, clutching the pen in her right hand.

It wasn't until she had almost reached the beginning of the Elgin property that she once again glanced at her watch and realized that she had been gone a long time. A much longer time than she had planned on when she sneaked out the back door.

She hurried on, sliding and scrambling on the steepest places and, on passing the border of saplings, scampering down the flights of stairs that led from one terrace to the next. On reaching the back door, she scarcely had time to put the pen in her pocket and pick up *Jane Eyre* and *Great Expectations* before the kitchen door opened and Hannah Abbott said, "Audrey. Where on earth have you been? I've been calling and calling."

"I didn't hear you," Audrey gasped breathlessly. "I was just . . ." She motioned vaguely toward the terraces and the hillside beyond. "Up where I go to read sometimes."

"To read?" The suspicious edge was there again as her mother's eyes turned toward the shelf where Audrey had left the books. Had she noticed that the books had been there the whole time Audrey was gone? She didn't say so. But her eyes were hinting something of the sort.

"Well, I *was* planning to read, but then I changed my mind and just went for a walk." She motioned again. "A long walk up the hill."

"I see. It must have been a long walk." Hannah Abbott wiped her hands on her apron, and as she turned away, she said, "I'm going to start dinner as soon as I finish the ironing. You're just in time to shell the peas."

Inside the kitchen, Audrey returned her father's grin and accepted a sloppy greeting from Beowulf before she started in on the peas. And it was that very evening, only a few minutes later, sitting right there at the kitchen table, when she suddenly found herself saying, "There's an old woman living in that cave where the Mayberry kids used to play."

And then her parents were agreeing that something had to be done about it, and her mother was saying she would call the police as soon as she finished ironing her blouse.

And that was only the beginning.

CHAPTER 7

AUDREY WAS SHELLING THE LAST FEW peas and frantically wondering what she should do to keep her mother from calling the police when Hannah Abbott calmly and methodically finished her blouse, put away the ironing board, and headed for the telephone. She was dialing the number when Audrey, still without any plan of action, said, "Mom, she doesn't need to be put in an institution."

Hannah stopped dialing and turned to look at Audrey without saying anything for a long moment—except with her eyes. "Why do you say that, Audrey?" she finally asked. "Why wouldn't there be something the authorities could do to help an old woman who's trapped in a cave on a steep hillside?"

Audrey shook her head. She didn't know why there was nothing the police could do, but she was sure that it was true. Looking into Hannah's narrowed eyes, she also knew what her mother was thinking.

"No, I'm not. I'm not making it up. She is there. It's just that she's not trapped or anything. I think she can leave whenever she wants to."

But now Hannah had turned her back and was dialing again and then saying hello and asking to talk to Captain Banner.

She talked on the phone for a long time, at least several minutes, speaking so softly that Audrey could make out only an occasional word or phrase. Things like "the cave on the hill" and "my daughter, Audrey." And later, sounding impatient, "I know, Captain Banner. I know."

At last she hung up the phone and turned to Audrey. "Captain Banner says the squad cars are out on call now, but he thinks someone can get up the hill as far as the cave sometime this evening." Her eyes narrowed again as she went on. "He promised to let me know what they've done about it." And there was nothing Audrey could do about it but shrug and hang her head so she wouldn't have to meet her mother's searching eyes.

Fortunately, her parents seemed to have a lot of other things to talk about at the dinner table that night. Mrs. Austin, her mother's boss at the savings and loan, the woman Audrey's father had nicknamed "The Warden," had been particularly rude and demanding lately, and some of the other clerks had been out sick so Hannah had lots of extra work to do.

And when Hannah had finished complaining about her bad week, it was John's turn, and what he brought up was a phone call they'd gotten from Dr. Richards. "The doc says we'd better just forget about the bypass operation. He says he's looked into it, and he thinks it's an unproven procedure with not a good enough track record."

Hannah shook her head, sighing. "I know," she said. "I was hoping so much that . . ." She sighed again and then lifted her chin and smiled weakly. "Well, we'll just keep on looking. There has to be something more someone can do."

Now and then Audrey tried to listen to what her parents were saying, but most of the time her mind was elsewhere. An elsewhere that included a steep, difficult climb, an almost hidden cave full of birds and bats, and a strange creature who was . . . what? Something terribly unusual, maybe something magical. And what would happen to her when the Greendale police tramped up the hill and burst into her cave?

Audrey had been certain all along that there wasn't anything the police could do that would help. But now she was becoming more and more sure that they might cause a lot of harm. As she pictured big old Captain Banner storming up the hill and stomping into the cave waving his baton and shouting, she became increasingly anxious and uneasy. Even when Beowulf put his head in her lap and rolled his eyes sympathetically, it didn't help. At least not as much as usual.

But it wasn't until dinner was finally over, with the table cleared and the dishwasher loaded, that Audrey escaped to her room and really began to fret. Standing at the window and looking up toward the darkening trail to the cave, she was overcome by a need to do something. To at least warn the woman that they would be coming. But how?

Could she get there in time? Before the police arrived? Probably not. And it was getting dark. Could she even find her way up the steep inclines and through the deeply shadowed groves at night? She didn't think so. And what if her mother called or came to her room while she was gone? And her father found out that she was missing? No, she couldn't risk that.

Back at her desk Audrey rested her head on her hands and closed her eyes. She sat that way for several minutes before she reached out and pulled her binder across the desk, then looked for a pencil or a pen. But her pencil tray was empty. She was starting to open another drawer when she suddenly remembered the pen in her pocket.

And then she was writing with the strange pen, writing hurriedly and hopelessly, but somehow feeling that she must. She wrote:

This is a warning. The police are coming to your cave, and it's my fault. I shouldn't have told anyone about you. I wish I could take you this note or maybe send it but

But what? What happened then? Afterward Audrey wasn't exactly sure, except that a while later, maybe only a few minutes, or perhaps longer, she was still sitting right there at her desk with the pen in her hand, but somehow feeling that she had been—where? Somehow she, or at least her mind, had been somewhere else, and now she was back and remembering how worried she had been feeling and how she had started writing. . . .

She sighed. *Yeah,* she thought. *That's me, all right. If I can't do anything that really matters, I just write about it.* She sat up straighter and took her hands off the page where she had been writing. She looked, then looked again. The page was blank and empty.

That was strange. She was sure she'd started writing— something. Something about a warning and the police. She could even remember how the words looked, smooth and dark, on the page of the notebook. But perhaps she had only imagined it.

Picking up the pen, she examined it carefully. The metal was a rusty reddish brown, like the fancy bronze vase that had belonged to her grandmother, and the marks that ran up and down the shaft looked almost like letters, but not any letters she'd ever seen before. Her writing had looked wide and heavy, as if the pen had a broad point, yet it seemed to come to a small roundish tip, like an ordinary ballpoint pen. But she was sure—well, almost sure—that she remembered seeing wide, dark lines. Pulling the notebook closer, she began to write again, starting with her name:

AUDREY ELGIN ABBOTT

The writing was easy, the point of the pen gliding smoothly over the paper. And, yes, the lines were wide and dark. She was still staring at the dark flowing letters when she began to feel . . . what? Something strange. Particularly strange under the circumstances. It was a calm, focused feeling that was somehow comforting even though it made no sense.

She shook her head, sighed, looked around, and then grinned. Of course—that was what, or who, was making her feel better: Beowulf had followed her to her room and was now standing near her chair, his big brown eyes looking at her sympathetically from only an arm's length away. Throwing her arms around his neck, she wrestled him to the floor. As usual, he pretended to growl and bite before he relaxed into a warm, comforting doggy pillow. And with her head on his shaggy back, Audrey collapsed too and, after a while, fell asleep.

Audrey didn't awake until much later, when her bedroom door opened and her mother said, "Well. Look at the two of you there on the floor, at this hour." She looked at her watch. "It's almost eleven o'clock." And then, as Audrey staggered to her feet, "Shall I take Beowulf out, or can you do it?"

"I will. I'll do it," Audrey said, and shaking her head to clear away the dream shadows, she whispered, "Come, Wulfy. Come."

As she trudged sleepily down the hall and then waited at the back door for Beowulf to take care of business, it all came back, and once again she was caught up in worry about what had happened or was going to happen at the cave. Had the police gone there? And what had they done when they were there? By the time she was back in her room and ready for bed, she had decided it must not have happened yet. It would be hard even for grown men with flashlights to get there in the dark, and besides, wouldn't her mother have said something if Captain Banner had already called back? She fell asleep still wondering, and it wasn't until she arrived in the kitchen the next morning that she found that she'd guessed correctly.

The police hadn't called the night before because they hadn't yet gone to the cave, but when the phone rang while Audrey was setting the table, it was Captain Banner calling for Hannah Abbott. Audrey gave the phone to her mother and then stood there with her hands full of forks and spoons while her mother talked and mostly listened. When Hannah finally hung up, she looked worried—and angry.

"Audrey," she said, shaking her head, "it's just what I

was afraid he'd tell me. Captain Banner says there wasn't anyone in the cave." She sighed, and Audrey knew what the sigh meant. It meant that Hannah Abbott believed that her daughter was either a liar or perhaps something even worse. Like a person who sees things that aren't really there.

Biting her lip and returning her mother's stare, Audrey tried to decide whether to argue. To insist that the woman had been there, so she must have heard the police coming and found a place, or a way, to hide. Or else that Captain Banner was probably just too lazy to make such a long climb and had just guessed at what he'd find. But she knew it would be useless. If Hannah Abbott wanted to believe she had a daughter who was either crazy or a liar, nothing anyone could say would make any difference.

CHAPTER 8

S O THAT WAS IT. NO ONE SAID ANYTHING more to Audrey about the woman in the cave, not even her father, although he certainly knew about Captain Banner's call and was worried about it, too. Several times that Monday, Audrey caught him watching her with his heavy, dark eyebrows at an anxious angle.

And what did Audrey do? Nothing. At least nothing that did any good. She thought, more than once, about bringing the subject up when she was alone with her father, but somehow she never did. She came close on Monday and again on Tuesday, after they'd played their usual chess game.

Perhaps she would begin by saying, *Look, Dad. I just want you to know that I didn't make that up about the woman in the cave. She really was there. And there was a duck, too, who came to lead me there. A big white duck. And there were other things in the cave, too. What other things? Oh, some owls and bats mostly, but also a lot of blackbirds.* She'd tell him all that, and then he might . . . No, she was afraid not.

When she was a little kid, her father had always been very understanding about her more or less improbable friends, like the closet ghost and the baby dragon. He'd always listened to her tell about them and asked serious questions, but that had been when she was five or six years old. If he did the same thing now it would probably mean that he was just humoring her because he, too, thought she had flipped out. And worrying about your only daughter going crazy certainly couldn't be very good for a person with a bad heart. So the safest thing to do was to go on saying nothing. Nothing at all, to anyone.

There was a brief moment on Wednesday when Audrey thought there might be another person she could talk to about some of the things that had been happening. It was during lunch hour when Audrey had picked up her tray in the cafeteria and was looking for a place to sit. A lot of classes were on field trips, so it wasn't as crowded as usual, and there, all by herself at a big table, was Debra Felton. Debra, sitting there all alone, then looking up and smiling and making a "come here" motion. Audrey turned around to look, but there was no one behind her, so Debra must have meant her. She was—well, surprised, to say the least—definitely surprised, and a little bit suspicious.

There had been a time, not all that long ago, when she might have said that the one person she could talk to about anything and everything, was Debra Felton. And now at lunch period on a sunny afternoon Debra was motioning for Audrey to sit at her table.

"Hi." Debra's blond eyebrows were jumping up and down the way they always did when she was really excited about something. "Hey. What's up, dude?"

Audrey returned her smile cautiously. "Nothing much," she said. "What's up with you?" She knew that the "dude" business and all the long strands of beads that Debra was wearing were because some of her new friends were kind of would-be hippies. Greendale Junior High didn't allow too much far-out stuff, but long necklaces made out of seeds and shells seemed to be all right. They were certainly okay with Audrey. She'd wear some herself if she had any. "I like your necklaces," she said to Debra. "Especially those seed things. They're sort of like some of the stuff . . ."

She let the sentence trail off, but Debra picked up on it. "Yeah, I remember. We used to grind up some seeds like this for our magic potions." The way she grinned and rolled her eyes when she said "magic potions" made it clear that she thought the whole thing had been pretty silly. "We were really weird, weren't we?"

"Yeah. Weird," Audrey agreed, at the same time thinking how dumb she'd been to think, even for a minute, that Debra would be a good one to tell about the woman in the cave.

"Hey, look." Debra looked at her watch and then at the

cafeteria door, probably hoping someone she'd rather talk to would come in. But maybe not, because the next thing she said was, "Some of us are planning to go hear the Sons of Champlin at the college tonight. Maybe you could go too?"

"The Sons of Champlin?" Audrey asked.

"Yeah, you know. The rock band. Mindy thinks they're the greatest. I was just thinking maybe you'd like to go too."

Audrey thought maybe she would, depending on . . . "When are you going?" she asked.

"Well, Tammy and Julie and their families are coming to my house about four o'clock. My folks are having a barbecue bash on our patio. And after the barbecue Mindy's mom is taking all of us kids to the J.C. Tell your mom that Mindy's mom is going to be there the whole time, so she doesn't have to worry about you running off to be a rock band groupie." She giggled and then gave Audrey a long look with her head cocked to one side. "You do want to go, don't you?"

Audrey nodded. "Sure, I want to," she said. "I'll ask." She did *want* to go, and that moment she was thinking she'd ask her father as soon as she got home. Then she could walk over to the Feltons' for the barbecue and go to the rock concert.

She thought about it all the way home—and by the time she got there, she'd changed her mind. She wasn't going to ask her father because she was pretty sure he'd say yes. He would say yes, and she would go to hear the Sons of Champlin. And while he was alone all afternoon, her father might . . .

So that day, like every other, she was home by one o'clock to play chess with her father, and do some homework while he read the papers. Then there was feeding Sputnik and cleaning his cage and a brief backyard trip with Beowulf before her mother came home. And, like always, it was almost eight by the time dinner was over and the kitchen cleaned up and Audrey was free to do—whatever she wanted. Whatever she wanted, that is, as long as it wasn't something that started before eight o'clock. So that pretty much narrowed down her free-time activities to going to her room to read. Or most likely to write, but not in her journal. Not tonight.

Audrey had found that journal writing could be useful. Not the deadly everyday kind where you wound up writing what you had for breakfast, but the kind where you only wrote about special times or feelings, good ones as well as bad. That kind of writing sometimes made good feelings last longer and bad ones seem less important. But for Audrey, the kind of writing that simply shoved everything else out of your mind—everything from a bad grade in math to not getting to go to the Sons of Champlin concert—was writing novels.

Digging down under a lot of old essays and math

papers in the bottom drawer of her desk, she pulled out the secret notebook where she kept all of the things she was still working on. One of the first manuscripts in the notebook was part of a fantasy she had started more than a year ago. A fantasy in which a strange, lily-shaped flower could turn anyone who touched it into an animal. Not any animal, but one who had some kind of relationship to the personality of the person who touched the flower. In some earlier chapters, she'd written about one character being changed into an elegant white swan. And most recently she'd gotten to where another character in the story, a really mean seventh-grade boy, had been transformed into a wild boar with a long, ugly snout and a curly tail.

For a while it had been a fun story to work on, but when she couldn't get it to head toward some more or less sensible ending, she had started a different one. Another mystery, but this time a more realistic one. But that had sputtered out too a few weeks ago, and she had gone on to the one about the girl detective who could solve mysteries by talking to animals.

That story had been going pretty well lately, and it had been during algebra that same morning that she'd just happened to come up with a new idea about how to get Heather out of the dangerous mess she had just gotten herself into.

Reaching into her pencil tray in her top drawer Audrey pulled out . . . the bronze pen.

CHAPTER 9

FOR A MOMENT AUDREY TURNED THE PEN this way and that, admiring its odd shape and color. She liked the look and feel of it, but what she'd really been looking for was a pencil. She never wrote her novels in ink because she'd found that being really original and creative meant doing a lot of erasing. She looked through the top drawer again, but all her pencils seemed to have disappeared. She sighed impatiently as she pawed through another drawer, and when Beowulf appeared in the doorway, she blamed it on him, even though he'd pretty much quit chewing on pencils when he'd lost his puppy teeth.

"Hey, monster dog," she said. "Did you take my pencils?" But Beowulf only nudged her with his nose, inviting her to wrestle. When she went back to looking through her desk drawers, he flopped down on the floor and went to sleep.

But Audrey was in a hurry. Right then—just when she

was going through her desk—she'd begun to come up with an even better way to solve the treacherous cat episode. The one in which the cat had talked Heather, the girl detective, into going down the alley where the murderer was lying in wait.

In this new version a large dog, perhaps an Irish wolfhound named . . . not Beowulf, but something just as brave and impressive sounding, like Hero, perhaps. Yes, Hero was going to come along and chase the cat up on top of a shed. And then the dog and the cat would start talking to each other, and with Heather's amazing ability to understand what animals were saying, she would learn the truth about the cat's evil plan and would be able to escape. To just barely escape, right when the murderer was emerging from his hiding place and was reaching out to grab her. It should be a very suspenseful episode.

It would be fun to write, too. She was good at dialogue, and a dialogue between a dog and a cat should be interesting. So she wouldn't waste any more time searching for pencils—the pen would have to do. She would simply scratch out any errors and plan on writing the whole thing over later to neaten it up.

Audrey began by rewriting the chapter title:

Heather's Alley Adventure

Once again, for the first few lines using the pen was a little distracting. The smooth flow of wide, dark lines was surprising and a bit intimidating. But as she went on writing, the look of the penned lines began to seem more natural.

Just as Heather started down the dark, sinister alley, she was suddenly aware of something cold and wet touching her elbow. It was a dog's nose. Not a dog she had ever seen before, but a large shaggy animal with friendly brown eyes.

"Hello, dog," Heather said. "Where did you come from, and who are you?"

"My name is Hero," the dog said, "and I'm here because I know that you can talk to animals. I want to talk to you. But please excuse me for a moment. There is something I must do first. Do you see that cat sitting on top of that shed?"

"Yes," Heather said. "That's the nice, friendly cat who said it would help me find my way home. He said I should follow him."

"Aha," the dog named Hero said. "That cat is lying to you. He belongs to a very evil man. That treacherous cat is leading you into deadly danger."

It turned out to be one of the best writing sessions that Audrey had had for a long time. The ideas just kept coming, and there were some scary parts and a few that were a little bit funny. It was really true that writing fiction was one of the best ways to cheer yourself up. Or, if not to actually make you cheerful, to at least make you forget the things that were worrying you.

The writing went on until she got to the place where Heather was about to be grabbed by the murderer, but because the dog called out a warning, she was able to escape by using a kick that she had learned from a chimpanzee who had studied karate.

It was an exciting climax, and Audrey was just finishing the chapter by describing how Heather called for the police to come pick up the unconscious murderer when she happened to glance at her watch and saw that it was after ten o'clock. Her mother would probably be coming in soon to take Beowulf out and say good night before locking up the house. And so, because she needed to be extra organized and responsible in order to reassure her parents about her mental condition, Audrey quickly got ready to be helpful.

Hurriedly stuffing her secret notebook back into its hiding place, she headed for the door, stopping only long enough to poke Beowulf with her toe to wake him up. He grunted and sighed, and then just as Audrey was turning the doorknob, he said, "What did you do that for?"

At least a rather gruff voice saying exactly that had come from someplace very nearby, and there was no one else in the room. Or maybe from right outside the door, although it didn't seem to come from that direction. Audrey carefully and quietly opened the door and peeked out into the hall. No one. Nothing in sight. Turning back, she stared at Beowulf, who was looking at her from under his shaggy eyebrows while he slowly rearranged himself so that his big paws were under him.

"Urff," he said as he struggled sleepily to his feet. A comment that had a reassuringly doggy sound. But then as Audrey turned back to reopen the door, he said clearly, "You didn't have to kick me."

Once again Audrey froze. She turned slowly back to where Beowulf was on his feet and moving toward her. Moving toward her and saying, "Okay, okay. It didn't hurt that much. Just don't do it again. Nice people don't kick their dogs."

Audrey shook her head and swallowed hard and stammered, "I—I didn't mean to kick you. I just gave you a poke with my toe."

"Okay, okay. Let's go. It's late. Let's get me outside before I make a big mistake."

They went down the hall side by side, a sleepy, floppy Beowulf and a stunned and staring Audrey. After crossing the kitchen, Beowulf stopped long enough to take a few laps from his water dish before he quietly, except for his padding feet and clicking toenails, headed for the back door. At that moment he was looking and acting normally doglike again, but Audrey watched him intently as she opened the door and stepped back out of the way. As he passed her he gave her wrist a sloppy kiss and, without saying another word, disappeared into the dark yard.

Audrey was still standing just inside the door—holding it slightly open, waiting for Beowulf to return, and desperately trying to make some sense out of what had just happened—when, from only a few feet away, someone said, "Will you shut that door! I'm freezing." It had to be Sputnik, but he was talking in a different way than usual. Instead of being high-pitched and squawky, his voice now sounded almost human.

Audrey was beginning to get the picture—or maybe a couple of equally confusing pictures. Either she really was flipping out or something exceptionally magical was happening. Something magical that was slowly becoming a little less shocking than it had seemed at first.

She seemed to be talking to animals. Doing something, *really* doing something, that she had imagined and even played at doing when she was a little kid. It was an idea that she'd fooled around with for a long time and had been using in the novel about the girl detective. And now it was, or at least it seemed to be, actually happening.

Leaving the door almost shut, she went closer to Sputnik's cage. The little gray and white parrot with bright orange circles on his cheeks was scrunched up against the far side of the perch, with his feathers fluffed up. Audrey spread her fingers out on the wires of the cage and leaned close.

"What a fussbudget," she said. "It's not that cold."

"You're wrong. You don't know anything," Sputnik said. "I'm a tropical bird. If you were tropical, you'd be freezing too."

Just then Beowulf shoved the door open, trotted in, and without making any other comments, headed for his crib mattress in the living room. Audrey quickly closed and locked the door and came back to Sputnik's cage. "There," she said. "Does that feel better?"

Sputnik made a snorting noise, flapped his wings, and sidled along his perch to where he could dip his beak into his food dish and flip seeds out onto the floor of his cage. There wasn't anything new or surprising about that. It had been a favorite activity of his ever since Audrey's father had saved him from the cruel reporter. But this time he stopped after five or six flips and, looking right at Audrey, said, "Look at that. All the good stuff is gone. All finished." Squinching his head down on his chest, he looked at Audrey out of the top of one eye and said, "And there wasn't that much of it to begin with."

Audrey inspected the contents of the feed dish. It did look as if the sunflower seeds, which he'd always seemed to prefer, had been eaten up.

"All right, I'll get you some more sunflower seeds," she

said, "if you promise not to peck me when I put them in your dish. Okay?"

Sputnik flapped his wings and screeched something in his usual cockatiel voice that sounded vaguely like "okay." Or maybe not. But whatever it was, he said it over and over again—"oke, oke, oke"—while Audrey got down the bag of sunflower seeds, took out a cupful, and proceeded to carefully open the door of the cage. While she filled the dish Sputnik went on screeching and bobbing his head up and down, but for once he didn't try to bite or to escape before she could close the door. So maybe he had been saying "okay" or something similar in cockatiel language.

When the door was safely shut and Sputnik was busy eating, Audrey went on standing in front of the cage, watching and wondering. She wondered about what she had heard or had seemed to hear. And after a while it occurred to her to wonder about something she hadn't heard. Leaning closer to the cage, she whispered, "Hey, Sputnik. How come no cussing?"

The cockatiel went on eating sunflower seeds. So she asked again. "What happened to all the cussing?"

Sputnik rolled a black eye in the direction of the feed dish, ate another sunflower seed, looked again, and then said, "I don't know. Maybe I ate it."

Audrey couldn't help laughing. "Cussing isn't something you eat. Cussing is all those bad words you always say." She whispered a couple of his favorites through the bars of his cage. "You know. Words like that."

Sputnik squawked and threw up his head in a threatening manner. "Those are yelling words. Anderson yelled them, so I yelled them back. That's just angry squawk-talk. Angry squawk-talk."

After Audrey thought about that for a minute, she began to feel really indignant. She'd never liked Andy Anderson much because when she used to visit her dad's office at the newspaper, he would always start to tell a joke and then think up a reason to send her out of the room before he got to the funny part. And now she was discovering that he himself had cussed at Sputnik, and when Sputnik cussed back, he named him Bleep and threatened to throw him out where the chicken hawks would get him.

"Well," she told Sputnik, "that's despicable. Anderson swore at you and then got mad at you for saying the same words. That's really despicable."

Sputnik did his aggressive strut, the way he always did when he was daring Beowulf to bite him. "Despicable," he said. "Despicable Anderson." But now he was using his cockatiel voice again, high-pitched and raspy.

He was still saying "despicable" several minutes later when Audrey left the kitchen.

CHAPTER 10

ON THE WAY BACK TO HER ROOM AUDREY was in a trancelike daze when she met her mother in the hall. "Oh, Audrey." Hannah looked tired and pale. "Did you take the dog out?"

Audrey must have said yes or at least nodded because her mother said, "Good for you. I almost forgot about him." She patted Audrey on the shoulder and turned away. Watching her go, it occurred to Audrey to think, *She didn't notice anything. So I must not look any different. The only difference is that now I can talk to animals.* She kept whispering it as she arrived at her room, got into her pajamas, and climbed into bed. Over and over again. "I can talk to animals. I can talk to animals." But after a while it sometimes came out, "I guess I can talk to animals. I guess I can, or else . . ." Or else what? Or else she really was going crazy.

Lying flat on her back with the covers pulled up to her

chin, she kept on saying one version and then the other. The "I can talk to animals" thing and then the "or else" version. But finally the words began to get slower and more muddled, and then it was morning and Audrey was waking up and asking herself if her talking-to-animals experience had really happened or if it had all been a particularly lifelike dream.

She couldn't help wishing that it would turn out to be a dream. Not that she wouldn't love to be able to talk to animals, but under the present circumstances all she needed was to go out and sit down to breakfast and, right there in front of her parents, start chatting up the family pets. That was all it would take for both of them, both her father and her mother, to be absolutely certain she was headed for the loony bin.

So a few minutes later it was with a great deal of nervous tension that Audrey entered the kitchen and sat down at her place at the breakfast table. Her parents were already there, and after they said hello, they went right on with their conversation about the new Doonesbury comic strip that had just started running in the *Greendale Times*. It was a topic that would have interested Audrey ordinarily, but this wasn't an ordinary morning.

As Audrey helped herself to the milk and cornflakes, she looked around quickly, checking on Sputnik and Beowulf. Beowulf was right there under the table, and Sputnik was admiring himself in his mirror. Neither of them was saying anything or paying any attention to what her parents were saying. It wasn't long before it became obvious that it was a good thing they weren't listening. Or at least that Beowulf wasn't, because the next topic of conversation turned out to be a newspaper article about some scientists who had been trying to repair damaged human hearts by using parts cut out of animals.

Audrey was shocked. As the conversation went on, it became clear that some of the hearts had been taken from pigs, but some others were from . . . *dogs*. Rearranging her chair so she could see Beowulf's face, she watched him closely for any sign of shock or alarm. Nothing. He was, Audrey decided, either too sound asleep to hear what her parents were saying or simply unable to understand.

By the time the meal was over, Audrey was feeling much less worried. In fact, she was beginning to think that it had been pretty ridiculous for her to think that Beowulf might have understood. After all, he'd never shown any signs of understanding what was being said before, unless one of his favorite words—words such as "good dog" or "walk"— happened to crop up. So what she'd heard last night was either some sort of hallucination or a temporary kind of magic that quickly came and went. And now it was gone.

That was the way she was feeling, anyway, until she took Beowulf on his morning outing. But after the back door had closed behind them and Beowulf had sniffed and piddled his way around the fence, like always, he came back, turned his big brown eyes in her direction, and said, "I knew it. That raccoon was here again last night."

Audrey stared. Stared, gulped, and said, "You can. You can talk."

"I can talk to you." Beowulf sat down in front of Audrey. "Sometimes I can." He held up a big front paw. "Shake," he said.

Audrey shook his paw. "But in there, in the kitchen just now . . . when my parents were talking. Did you understand what they were saying?"

Beowulf tipped his head to one side and looked thoughtful. "No. Not them."

"And how come you didn't talk to me when we were in there, but now you are? Why is that?"

Beowulf sighed thoughtfully and lifted his other front paw. "Mostly I want to talk, but I don't know how. Maybe I only can when something tells me how."

As she shook Beowulf's other paw, she said, "I guess you're right. I don't understand it either, but I think you're right."

So that was the way things stood all through Thursday. Audrey went to school and then came home, and the only conversation that went on was between Audrey and her father, except for an occasional parrot-type comment from Sputnik. There was one big difference there, however. Sputnik seemed to have stopped swearing.

His other familiar comments were the same as ever.

He still squawked "Hello, hello" and "Shut up" and "Polly want a martini" and some other stuff that Mr. Anderson had taught him. But no more long strings of cuss words. And nothing at all in the more human-sounding voice that he'd used the night before.

And nothing more that evening, either, while Dr. Richards was there. Dr. Rob Richards, who was an old friend and neighbor as well as the Abbotts' family doctor, often stopped by in the evening. And on that particular night he stayed quite late, sitting at the kitchen table with all of the Abbotts and talking about politics, Greendale gossip, and John Abbott's heart. And all that time Sputnik made only parrot-type comments and Beowulf said nothing at all.

But only a little while later, when John and Hannah were seeing Dr. Richards to the door and Audrey came through the kitchen on her way to take Beowulf out, Sputnik once again reminded her not to leave the door open. And a few minutes after that, when she came back in, he stopped scattering birdseed long enough to say, "How about some more of the good stuff?"

But that was it. By Friday it all seemed to have ended. After that when Audrey managed to be alone with one or both of them from time to time, neither Beowulf nor Sputnik had anything to say.

For a while Audrey thought about it constantly and wondered why it had happened—and then had stopped happening. But as the days passed, she began to have other things to worry about. Like, for instance, what her next report card was going to look like. It wasn't until she'd been called in to talk to the student adviser that she realized how careless she'd been lately about doing some assignments and studying for a couple of tests.

"Your teachers tell me this isn't like you," Mrs. Bishop, the adviser, said. "Your grades have always been excellent, and now they seem to be going down quite rapidly." After straightening up her notes, she leaned forward and put her hand on Audrey's shoulder and asked, "Is there anything on your mind that you'd like to talk about, dear?"

There wasn't. Not a chance. No chance that she was going to start explaining how what had been on her mind was a strange creature she'd seen in a cave on Wild Oaks Hill or how Beowulf and Sputnik had suddenly turned into conversationalists.

But when Audrey assured Mrs. Bishop that she was all right and that she was sure she could bring her grades back up very quickly, she really meant it. After all, right then, when her parents were already pretty sure she was either telling lies or having hallucinations—or both—it would be a bad time for them to get a report card that showed that she was falling apart in English and math, too.

So for the rest of that week and the one that followed, Audrey was so busy working on her math and writing overdue essays that she had very little time to worry about anything else. It wasn't until the essays were completed and she had done well on one or two math assignments that she once again had time to worry about some of the weird things that had happened, or seemed to have happened, in the recent past. Not that she wanted to go back to lying awake nights thinking about what the strange creature in the cave had told her or what Beowulf and Sputnik had said in perfect English. Two subjects that were going to be hard to avoid unless ... unless she could get her mind completely focused on something else, like a new novel, for instance.

BUT WHAT NOVEL SHOULD IT BE? THERE still was the one about the girl detective, but Audrey had finished the chapter about the evil cat in the sinister alley, and after quite a bit of thought no other exciting possibilities had come to mind. And the earlier story about the magical transforming lily had bogged down where the main character, a stuck-up jerk, had managed to get himself turned into a wild boar.

However, she had been thinking about a slightly interesting idea she'd gotten from Mr. Baxter's list of extra-credit projects for English class. A list that had included such uninspiring suggestions as interviewing an important Greendale citizen and then writing their biography. An interview with Captain Banner, for instance? No thanks.

But there was one extra-credit project that had caught Audrey's attention. And that was writing and illustrating a picture book for beginning readers.

While she had never thought of herself as a really gifted artist, she was able to draw some things pretty well, and as for the story itself . . . Well, writing a picture-book story should be no problem for an experienced novelist, even one who was not exactly well known. At least, not yet.

So it was a little after eight o'clock on a moonlit night in May that Audrey sat down at her desk, opened her novel notebook, and got ready to write a very short story. But after half an hour or so she was still staring at the blank paper. It was beginning to seem that most of the good ideas that might appeal to little kids had already been done. But finally, after a lot of wasted time and paper, she began to get an interesting idea.

It was an idea that came out of her own life, when she was about as old as the readers of the book would be. She could write a story about a baby dragon who lived under the main character's bed. A character who would be a little girl who might be called . . . Let's see. Perhaps Debby? Then a nice alliterative title for the book could be *Debby's Dragon*.

So she wrote *Debby's Dragon* at the top of one page of her secret notebook, and then, with her pencil poised, she stared at the two words and waited for a good beginning sentence to come to mind. But for quite a long time nothing did. After a while she decided the problem had something to do with the title. Somehow the look of the thin lead-gray letters scribbled across the top line of a sheet of notebook paper wasn't all that inspiring, particularly when you compared it to the way her handwriting looked when she was using ... Suddenly she put down the pencil, opened her top drawer, and got out the bronze pen and several sheets of white construction paper. She folded the paper so each sheet made four pages of a very small book, and using the bronze pen, she wrote across the top of the first page, in careful block printing:

DEBBY'S DRAGON
By Audrey Abbott

And right away the ideas began to flow as smoothly and easily as the lines made by the bronze pen. On the first page she wrote:

Debby liked to think about dragons and play that she could see them. Beautiful dragons who could fly and shoot fire out of their noses.

"Nostrils" would sound more elegant, but since "nostrils" probably wouldn't be in a first grader's reading vocabulary, "noses" would have to do. The story went on:

In her room Debby had lots of dragon pictures and toy dragons, too.

Actually, the dragons in Audrey's collection, which she still kept on the top shelf of her bookcase, weren't the kind of things you'd call "toys." More like figurines. Dragon figurines. But once again a simpler word would be better for a beginning reader. The next page read:

> She had silver dragons and wooden dragons and dragons made out of glass.

Since there couldn't be much writing on each page, in order to leave room for a picture, the written part of the book had to be very brief. And drawing the pictures should be quick and easy too. At one time Audrey had spent a lot of time drawing dragons. She remembered using crayons and colored pencils to sketch bulging eyes, long scaly bodies, and billowing clouds of smoke and flame. The pictures would be fun. But the writing began to get a little more complicated when she arrived at the next part of the story.

> But Debby had a secret. In her room, along with the toy dragons, there was one real live dragon. A very young dragon who sometimes hid under her bed.

The problem was that Audrey wanted to describe the dragon as she used to imagine him when she was little, but in words that an ordinary first grader could read and understand. That might not be so easy.

You might be able to say, for instance, that the dragon was mostly green, except for his purple face and feet, and most first graders would probably understand how a baby dragon who tried to breathe fire usually only managed a warm hiccup and a pale puff of smoke. But it wouldn't be so easy to explain that he only pretended to be dangerous and sinister. Although he was good at lying in wait and lunging out fiercely, you only had to shout or stamp your foot and he whimpered and crawled back under the bed.

Audrey thought of several different versions, but none of them were exactly right. It was hard to describe her imaginary dragon without using words like "anxious" and "insecure"—words that she herself wouldn't have been able to read when she was five years old. But in those days she hadn't needed words to understand her dragon, and when she'd told her father about him, he seemed to understand too. To understand that while having a live-in dragon might be a little bit weird, it really wasn't all that dangerous.

Translating a not-very-typical dragon into first-grade English turned out to be not that easy, but Audrey finally thought she'd gotten the idea across pretty well. She was running out of pages when she finally came up with a fairly good ending. The last page of the book read:

Debby and her baby dragon went on being almost friendly for a long time. Until the dragon got too big to hide under the bed and Debby got too old to imagine him so well. Then he went away.

Audrey wasn't entirely satisfied with the ending, but she would wait until later to decide whether it needed to be rewritten. And then would come the drawing of the illustrations. Putting the unfinished book in her school binder, she got ready for bed.

CHAPTER 12

IT WAS VERY LATE, PERHAPS ONE OR TWO o'clock in the morning, when, very suddenly, Audrey was awake. Wide awake and wondering what she had just heard—and felt. She was just beginning to relax, thinking that she probably had only been having a very vivid dream, when it happened again. This time her bed definitely went up and then down, as if it were being moved by a slight earthquake. Or else being shaken by somebody— or something. Blinking the sleep from her eyes, she looked carefully from side to side.

The full moon sifting in through the window curtains produced enough light so that she was able to see that no one was standing by her bed, and propping herself up on her elbows, she was able to determine that there was no one anywhere else in the room. She was breathing a sigh of relief and starting to relax when the thumping came again—and then once more. Wide awake now,

Audrey began to realize exactly where it was coming from. Something was under the bed and bumping against the mattress. Something that must be rather large and strong. Much larger, at least, than a mouse or even a rat. No little rodent could shake the bed like that. *Beowulf?* she wondered hopefully. But, no. Beowulf could never squeeze his one hundred and fifty pounds under such a low bed.

Another thump and, at the same time, a scuffling, scratching noise. A noise that seemed to be moving toward the left side of the bed. Scooting to the right as far as she could, Audrey sat bolt upright, staring in the direction of the sound and seeing nothing but the edge of the bed and, beyond that, only moonlit curtains. And then ... And then, slowly stretching up into sight, two long, slightly curved plumes came into view, distinctly silhouetted against the moonlit windows. Feathery plumes that looked like the feelers of a moth or a butterfly, only much larger and longer. The limber feelers bent and turned and then raised up higher as something else came into view. Just below the feelers two other objects appeared. The wings of a very large bat? No. More like dark, spiky ears. The ears twitched back and forth and moved higher, and then, just below them, Audrey was able to make out a rounded dome, down the middle of which ran a row of sharp-looking spines. The dome turned, raised up higher, and she was staring into two round, glowing holes at the end of a long snout and, just above them, two bulging golden eyes.

She gasped. Pulling the covers up almost to her own eyes, she cowered back against the head of the bed and watched as the dragon's head—it was now obvious that's what it had to be—raised up higher, and higher still, on a long, limber neck. A very long neck that kept stretching up higher and higher until two skinny legs appeared. Legs that ended in large claws that curled down to sharply pointed talons.

Audrey gasped again, and the dragon suddenly noticed her. It jerked back, and the glowing holes at the end of its long, thin muzzle released, not a rush of flame so much as a brief fiery flicker, followed by a small puff of white smoke.

In spite of the fact that she kept trying to tell herself that it was only a dream, Audrey was frightened. *A dream* she told herself firmly. *I must be dreaming about my old pretend dragon.* But there was a part of her mind that wasn't accepting that explanation. A part that kept bringing up the fact that this creature was a lot more explicitly dragonlike than anything her five-year-old mind had ever been able to produce. Her preschool imagination had been pretty creative, but it had never conjured up such details as the glaring golden eyes and spiky ears that Audrey was now able to see so clearly, or the way the claws curled down to end in such long, sharp spikes. A dragon who probably wouldn't be so easily discouraged as the one created by a five-year-old's imagination. But then again, perhaps it would be worth a try.

Suddenly dropping the sheet she'd been clutching, Audrey leaned forward, clapped her hands sharply, and said, "Shoo!"

It worked. Jerking its head up and back, the dragon made a startled-sounding "Oooff," and ducked down to disappear from sight. And a moment later Audrey felt, once again, the scratching and thumping that had awakened her. The thumps continued for several seconds, became less noticeable, and stopped. Stopped altogether—for a minute, and then for several more.

Do dragons sleep? Perhaps not, but then again . . . Audrey went on straining her ears to listen. Nothing. No sound at all, but no sleep for Audrey, either. Lying wide awake, she listened and waited, wondering what had really happened and what she ought to do about it.

She thought briefly of getting out of the bed and looking under it. *Very* briefly. The dragon had been too real, too distinctly seen. But at last she did do something. Clutching a blanket, she stood up, breathlessly gathered her courage, and jumped. Jumped toward the door, snatched it open, and kept going. Out the door and down the hall to wind up on the couch in the living room next to where Beowulf was sprawled out on his baby crib mattress. He woke up only long enough to watch Audrey arrange the couch's pillows and her one skimpy blanket into a more or less comfortable bed, and went back to sleep without commenting beyond a sleepy grunt.

By the time she woke up the next morning, feeling a bit cramped and chilly, Audrey could look back at what had happened in a more realistic way. It obviously had been a dream. An extremely realistic and vivid dream that perhaps had been brought about by the fact that, in writing *Debby's Dragon,* she had spent so much time and effort trying to remember the imaginary dragon of her childhood. And perhaps succeeding in remembering it in such great detail only because, as a little kid, she really had possessed a hyperactive imagination.

Back then she had made up all sorts of particulars about the baby dragon, and all sorts of other things, too, including many extra facts about the Mayberry twins' pirates. Besides what James had told her, Audrey had added such details as hooked noses, evil squinty eyes, and black jagged teeth. Enough scary details so that, back then in the days of the pirate game, she often had half-asleep dreams that were pretty nightmarish. So it was no wonder that her dream about a dragon could be full of more convincing details than the average person might experience. It was a somewhat comforting thought.

Comforting enough, at least, to make it possible for her to scoot back into and out of her room that morning to get her clothes and the books she would need for school. After dressing quickly in the bathroom, she arrived in the kitchen in time to set the table for breakfast.

By the time school was over that day, and an afternoon

spent, as usual, with her father, Audrey was no longer worrying about the dragon under her bed. Not much, anyway. But enough so that when dinner was over, she told her parents that she had finished her homework, which was true, and since she was only planning to read, she might just as well do it right there, with them, in the living room.

When her parents looked a little surprised, she explained by blaming it on the full moon. "Yeah," she said, grinning, "I guess I just don't like being alone when the moon is full."

As usual, her father made it into a joke. "I see," he said. "In case you start turning into a werewolf? Thanks for the warning." He rolled his eyes from side to side as if frantically looking for something. "Where did I put that gun with the silver bullets?"

So that took care of the evening, and when it was bedtime, Audrey waited until she was sure her parents were in bed before she tiptoed into her room, grabbed a blanket—a warmer one this time—and headed for the living room couch.

CHAPTER 13

THE NEXT DAY WAS THURSDAY, ONE OF the days when Audrey had art for her elective period. She'd always liked to draw and paint, but in this particular class Miss Joyce, the instructor, never seemed very interested in anything that Audrey had done. So when Audrey showed her the not-yet-illustrated picture book she'd made for her extra-credit project in English, she wasn't expecting much. But Miss Joyce was surprisingly enthusiastic. After she leafed through Audrey's dragon story, she said that it was a well-conceived project and that she really liked the little twist at the end.

"What are your plans for the illustrations?" she asked. "Lots of little dragons, I should think. What medium are you thinking of using?" She fingered one of the pages. "I don't think this paper could handle watercolors."

"Well, maybe I could use—," Audrey was saying when

someone else interrupted with, "How about ink and then poster paint?"

Up until that moment Audrey had been only vaguely aware that the girl who was standing on the other side of Miss Joyce's desk was listening. A girl whose unfamiliar face meant that she must be new to Greendale Junior High. Not that Audrey knew everybody at school, at least not well, but the person who had just suggested poster paint wasn't the kind to be easily forgotten. Tall and closer to skinny than slim, she had golden brown skin and eyes and a wild mop of curly black hair. And now she was leaning closer, looking at Audrey's book and asking, "Dragons?" And then adding, "Dragons are one of my specialties."

"Is that so?" Miss Joyce said. "That's an interesting coincidence, isn't it?"

From there, the conversation got rather involved, but it wound up with Miss Joyce suggesting that, since Lizzie—the new girl's name was Lizzie Morales—probably wouldn't have time to do an extra-credit project of her own before the deadline, she might be able to help Audrey finish hers.

"Would that be all right with you?" Miss Joyce asked Audrey.

So of course Audrey had to say it would be, even though she wasn't too pleased with the idea, at least not right away. She wasn't sure just why, except that the dragon picture book project had been inspired by a fairly private part of her life. Personal things were involved, like her silly childhood game, a recent nightmare, and a lot of years of dealing with what might be called an overactive imagination. None of which she was going to discuss with anyone, whether they happened to be dragon experts or not. But she couldn't help being a little curious.

"How did you get into dragons?" she asked the new girl.

With wide-eyed sincerity, Lizzie said, "Oh, I'm related to a lot of them." Then she grinned. "Just kidding. Mostly by reading about them, I guess. I've read lots of books about dragons. My favorite is *Dragonquest* by Anne McCaffrey. Have you read it?"

"Sure," Audrey said. "I liked it too. But . . ." She hesitated. There was one small problem. Enormous flying dragons who soared through the sky, shooting out deadly sheets of fire, didn't seem to be that closely related to the dragon in Audrey's story.

"But?" Lizzie asked, so Audrey tried to tell her that the dragon in her story was small and rather timid. "He's just very young, I guess," she finished. "Like, just hatched, maybe."

"Oh, well." Lizzie looked disappointed. "I haven't drawn any hatchlings." She thought for a moment before she added, "Couldn't you change the plot a little? Would it be too hard to write it over and make the dragon a little more like—like one of . . . Wait, I'll show you."

Opening a big, bulgy leather briefcase, she pulled out an apple and a squashed sandwich, which she dumped on the floor, and went on pawing through the contents of the oversized piece of luggage. She had added a binder, two or three books, and a beat-up pair of sneakers to the pile before she came up with a portfolio full of drawings.

Some of the pictures looked a bit ragged and dog-eared and had an odd smell. Tuna sandwich, perhaps, or dirty gym shoes—or both. All of that first bunch, even the dog-eared smelly ones, turned out to be very professional-looking caricatures of famous people. A little bit cartoonish, but easily recognizable pictures of Elvis Presley, all four of the Beatles, and even one of Queen Elizabeth.

Audrey was impressed, and Miss Joyce seemed to be even more so. "Did you really draw these yourself?" she asked, leafing through the stack.

Lizzie nodded and, looking a little uneasy, reached out trying to substitute another stack for the caricatures. "Those aren't the right ones," she said. "Here. Here are the dragons."

But Miss Joyce had just come across an especially interesting portrait of a man with horns and a long pointed tail whose lumpy, long-nosed face managed to look a little like—actually quite a lot like—Mr. Spaulding, the principal of Greendale Junior High.

"And this is . . . ?" Miss Joyce asked, obviously trying to hide a smile.

"Nobody. Nobody real," Lizzie said, quickly taking the devilish Mr. Spaulding away and handing Miss Joyce the other stack. "*Here* are the dragons," she insisted. This time the picture on top was a drawing of a typically terrifying McCaffrey-type dragon carrying a handsome dragon-rider on his back and spouting a sweeping plume of fire and smoke. "There. Like that," Lizzie said. "Wouldn't a dragon like that make the book a little more exciting?"

The picture was beautifully drawn and full of realistic details, but it certainly wasn't Audrey's dragon. And for some reason she felt it wouldn't be right to dump her baby dragon in favor of such a scary looking fire-breather. At least not in a book for little kids. But the only sensible argument she could come up with was, "Yeah, sure. But don't you think that kind of dragon might a little *too* exciting for first graders?"

"Well, yeah," Lizzie said, grinning. "You might be right. Might scare their little pants off."

Encouraged, Audrey went on. "And besides," she said, pressing her advantage, "I don't have my special pen with me. The one I used to do the book. I'd have to use it if I did the book over."

Lizzie pulled the book closer and examined the smooth, dark lettering Audrey had done with the bronze pen. She looked at it for quite a while, turning the pages and tipping the book from side to side. "Yeah, I see what you mean." She moved the little book over to compare it to the handwriting on the penciled notes in Audrey's binder. "Using that pen does do a lot for your . . ." She let her voice trail off into silence, leaving Audrey with a real need to know what she had been about to say.

"Does a lot for my what?" she asked urgently.

Lizzie looked up quickly and stared at Audrey. "For your handwriting," she said finally. "What else?" She sighed. "Okay, I'll tame my fire-breather down a little, but not too much. I don't do Disney-type dragons. Okay?"

Audrey wasn't convinced, at least not until she saw the first fairly innocent but definitely not-Disneyish-looking dragon that Lizzie came up with. Still not exactly cuddly-looking, but somehow much more like the one in Audrey's story.

"Okay?" Lizzie asked. And when Audrey nodded uncertainly, Lizzie added, "All right. We're in business. Gimme five." Audrey put out her hand, and Lizzie slapped it, before she started drawing her version of Audrey's dragon on each page of the book.

On the page about the dragon figurines, or toy dragons, she made a scattering of tiny dragonets that really did look as if they were made from glass or plastic. And then there was Audrey's baby dragon again, crawling out from under a bed, and crouching against a wall, looking hopefully ferocious.

As soon as Lizzie finished a drawing, Audrey began painting it in, blending shades of blue and green and purple, punctuated by golden eyes and nostrils. The overall effect was pretty impressive. They weren't quite finished by the time the period was over, but when Audrey and Lizzie showed Miss Joyce what they'd accomplished, she was even more complimentary.

Back at home that afternoon Audrey decided, after some thought, to let her father see the nearly finished book and tell him about the new girl named Lizzie and what had happened in art class. The reason she had some misgivings about telling him was, of course, because he'd heard about her dragon before. Maybe seven or eight years ago when she used to tell him how she pretended, and almost believed, that a dragon lived under her bed. And she certainly didn't want him to think she still . . . But on the other hand, she guessed that John Abbott would like hearing about Lizzie and the whole art class episode. It was a good guess.

"Very nice job," he said when he'd finished looking through the book. "Ought to be a bestseller." He grinned. "And this Lizzie is quite an amazing artist. And something of an original herself, I think? True?"

"True," Audrey agreed.

That night Audrey decided to sleep in her own bed for the first time since the return of the baby dragon, and except for a brief scratching noise that quickly died away, nothing at all happened.

CHAPTER 14

THE EXTRA CREDIT AUDREY GOT FOR HER picture-book project might make a real difference in her English grade, or it might not. But getting to know Lizzie Morales started making some differences right away. In art class on Tuesday she moved her desk next to Audrey's, and on Wednesday she was waiting for Audrey outside the cafeteria at lunch hour. For the next few days lunch became a few minutes of eating together and forty minutes of Audrey watching Lizzie draw pictures. Pictures of people in the lunchroom, of famous people, and then of people in Lizzie's family. Lizzie came from a large family, parents and grand-parents as well as a whole lot of older siblings, so that took a couple of days all by itself.

Lizzie did a lot of complaining about her family—how impossible it was for her to have any privacy and how, as the youngest, she never got to make any decisions. And how having a lot of older brothers was a real pain in the "you know where."

. She did have one sister, she told Audrey, but she was just a different kind of pain. "She's a whole lot older than I am." When Audrey asked how old, Lizzie shrugged. "I don't know. At least sixty-five." She grinned. "She acts like it, anyway. Actually, she just had her nineteenth birthday. But we have to share a room, and she's a real neatnik, and I'm definitely not. We drive each other crazy."

But when Audrey tried to sympathize, Lizzie grinned and said, "Well, I guess it could be worse. The whole family does so much yelling at each other that when they get around to yelling at me, they're usually pretty much out of breath."

When Lizzie asked about Audrey's family she told her a little about her mother's lousy job, where her boss hated her because she was so beautiful. "At least that's what my dad says," Audrey said.

When Lizzie asked, "And what does your dad do?" Audrey only said her dad was sick and let it go at that.

It was about two weeks after they'd met that Lizzie announced that she would like to be invited to visit.

"To visit?" Audrey said, and then asked stupidly, "Visit what?"

"Your house?" Lizzie made it into a question. "Like, where you live?"

At least Audrey didn't make it worse by asking why, but

Lizzie went on to explain: "I guess I'm just curious to see what it's like being an only child. I haven't a clue. Missed out on that one by a whole lot. And you know what? Up until now I've never even had a best friend who was one."

Audrey had mixed feelings. She kind of liked hearing that Lizzie thought they were best friends. But as for visiting at each other's homes, Audrey didn't know. It had been more than a year since she'd pretty much stopped asking friends over. Mostly because her mother thought that having extra kids around might be too stressful for her dad, but also because the whole atmosphere at the Abbotts' nowadays seemed to make most of her friends uneasy. So she hedged a bit by reminding Lizzie that she always went home early.

"Well, you couldn't come home *with* me. Not unless you wanted to ditch a couple of classes," she said. But Lizzie quickly replied that she could come later by herself if Audrey would tell her which buses to take. Audrey couldn't think of any other excuses, so it was about three thirty on a Friday afternoon when Lizzie Morales arrived at the Abbotts' house.

Audrey, who'd been waiting in the living room, heard the front gate creak open. She went to the hall window and watched Lizzie trudging up the walk, carrying her huge lumpy briefcase.

Audrey had warned her about Beowulf, of course, but for a lot of people being forewarned wasn't enough to prepare them for an enthusiastic Irish wolfhound greeting. But when Beowulf did his usual bouncy welcoming ceremony, complete with lots of sloppy kisses, Lizzie seemed delighted. And when Audrey introduced her to John Abbott, she said hello in an easy, unembarrassed way, which, in Audrey's experience, was hard for some people to do when they met someone in a wheelchair.

The first thing John Abbott said was, "Well, young lady. I must say I'm very impressed by your artistic talent." And everything that was said after that was pretty much on the same theme. Lizzie got her portfolio out of her briefcase, and the three of them went through all her drawings, the dragons as well as the caricatures. Audrey's father was particularly interested in the caricatures.

At one point he went through the morning newspaper picking out people for Lizzie to draw. People like President Nixon and Golda Meir, both of whom Lizzie said were easy, because to do a good caricature, you need subjects who have features that are easy to exaggerate. And, according to Lizzie, both the president and the prime minister of Israel had noses that were naturally exaggerated. Lizzie sat down on the floor by the coffee table, and in a few minutes, she quickly and easily did recognizable sketches of them both.

There was also a picture of Laurence Olivier in the *Greendale Times* that day, but Lizzie said he would be harder to caricature because he was handsome. That was when Audrey pointed to her father and said, "Can you do one of him?"

Lizzie looked at John Abbott from one side and then walked around to the other. "Not that easy, but I can try."

So she sat back down at the coffee table and began to draw. It didn't take her long, and when she was through, there was a sketch of a man with a thin face, high cheek bones, and slanted eyebrows who, like John Abbott, managed to be kind of handsome without looking like Clark Gable or any other movie star.

When she was done, Audrey said, "Yeah. Looks just like him," and her dad said, "Well, maybe. Twenty years ago."

After that Lizzie put all her stuff away in her briefcase and said she would have to leave soon. But before she did, she wanted to meet Sputnik. "I'd like to see your dragon collection too," she said. "I'll bet we have some of the same ones."

After Audrey's dad went to his room to rest, Audrey and Lizzie went to the kitchen to see Sputnik, who wasn't in a very talkative mood, but he did do his "Polly-wants-a-martini" thing when Audrey asked him to.

When Lizzie asked if he said anything else, Audrey answered, "He used to say a whole lot of swear words because my dad got him from a man who swore. But now he seems to have forgotten most of them."

"Oh yeah?" Lizzie said. "That's too bad." Putting her face up close to Sputnik's cage, she asked him if he'd forgotten something. "Come see me, pretty boy," she said. "Five minutes with my brothers and it would all come back."

Then they went to Audrey's room to look at her collection of dragons. After they took all the figurines off the top shelf and put them on Audrey's desk, Lizzie inspected each one very carefully. There were a couple, one of spun glass and one of china, that Lizzie said were exactly the same as hers. "Another coincidence," Lizzie said significantly, and Audrey agreed, and it wasn't until later that she wondered why. Except for liking dragons, what other coincidences did a short, pale only child and secret author have with a tall, dark artist who came from a huge family and who wasn't a bit secretive about her special talent?

Audrey was still having mixed feelings about the whole thing that evening when, back in her room, she looked at some of the pictures Lizzie had drawn that afternoon and thought about how enthusiastic her dad had been about them. Sitting at her desk, Audrey picked up the picture of her dad that Lizzie had drawn, trying to figure out just which lines made it be John Abbott and not any other man with high cheekbones and tilted eyebrows. Getting out some unlined paper, the kind she'd used for the picture book, she picked up a pencil and began to draw. But it was no good. Even with Lizzie's picture right there to copy, she wasn't able to draw a good likeness. Or even a good caricature.

After a while she started wondering if her dad would be as enthusiastic about her stories as he was about Lizzie's drawings, if and when she decided to let him read them. Probably not, she decided, even though what she did required a large amount of talent too. Talent that certainly should be obvious to anyone who took the time to read her stories carefully. Which her parents might do, if and when she decided to let them.

Audrey dug out her novel notebook and began to go through it, reading bits and pieces of things she'd written and imagining how certain readers might react to some of the best parts.

She looked at some of the older stories first—ones she'd written in the fifth and sixth grades. Not too bad, she decided. Not great maybe, but, of course, she'd been younger when she wrote stuff like that.

She flipped through a few more pages until she came to the girl detective story. The one about the girl who could talk to animals. Reading over some of the scene about Hero, the dog who came to the rescue, particularly the dialogue between Heather and Hero, she thought she'd managed to make the dog sound intelligent and yet realistically doglike. It really was, she decided, pretty good writing. Good enough that a person who knew about such things—for instance, someone who had been a newspaper editor—should recognize that it showed real talent.

Turning a few more pages, she stopped where she'd

started working on the book for first-grade readers. There wasn't much there, just the title—*Debby's Dragon*—written in ordinary pencil. Because after that she'd made the little book out of construction paper and started using the bronze pen. And the result had been the picture book that was still displayed on Mr. Baxter's bulletin board with an A+ grade written in red pencil on the first page.

So using the bronze pen had resulted in a good extra-credit grade in English class. Audrey was beginning to wonder if there had been other, more mysterious results. Marking her place in the notebook, Audrey closed it, opened the top drawer of her desk, and took out the bronze pen.

CHAPTER 15

IT WASN'T THE FIRST TIME SHE'D STUDIED the pen carefully, wondering about the significance of its metallic red-gold color and the letterlike markings that circled down its length. The strange way it felt in her hand—heavy without being clumsy or hard to use— and the way its narrow pointed tip produced such a smooth, wide line. Opening her notebook to a fresh page, she wrote . . . nothing, for quite a long time, while she tried to decide just how to begin. At last, just to see how the letters and numbers flowed out in that wide, smooth way, she wrote the date:

May 25, 1973

The idea she'd started to fool around with was that writing with the pen might have had something to do with some of the unusual things that had been happening. It was almost as if all she had to do was write about something with the pen and it would come true, or at least some part of it would. But if that was so, and if there really was something very special about the pen, maybe even magical, why had it been given to her?

There was only one person who might be able to answer all those questions, and she had gone away. At least she had not been in the cave when the police went there to look for her. But then again, wasn't it possible that she had returned in the same mysterious way she had made herself disappear? And if Audrey could visit the cave just one more time, wasn't it possible that the old woman might be able to explain some of it? Or even all of it?

Of course, the problem—and it was a big one—was the visiting part. She had been forbidden to go there again, and she had, more or less, promised that she wouldn't. But if she could somehow make a very short visit, without going there in the ordinary slow and difficult way, wouldn't that make it okay? Suddenly letting the point of the pen drop down onto the paper Audrey wrote in very large letters:

The Cave
I want to go

She got that far before she stopped writing and, with the pen still in her hand, got up and went to the window.

It was a sinister night. Thick clouds hung heavy in the sky, and beyond the glass the night was deadly dark, alive only with the sound of wind. The kind of wind that blinded your eyes and deafened your ears with its angry roar. She stood there for a long time looking out into the flowing, moaning darkness. Not a good time to go anywhere, and yet . . . She went on arguing with herself until she suddenly remembered a fact that helped her come to a decision. She would put the pen away and wait for daylight before she wrote anything more.

The fact that Audrey had remembered was that tomorrow morning her parents would be going to Dr. Richards's office. Usually Audrey went with them on those Saturday-morning appointments, and she either sat in the car and read or went to the library, until it was time to have lunch with her parents at the clinic's cafeteria. But if she could convince them to let her stay home, it would be a good time to try to find out if . . . If what? If there was any truth to the crazy idea she had begun to fool around with.

Her plan worked. Oh, her mother objected at first, as Audrey had known she would. "You know I don't like to leave you alone in the house for such a long time," she said.

"Oh, I'll be fine," Audrey told her, and then grinned as she added, "Beowulf will protect me." That was a laugh, and they all did, even Audrey's mom. Anyone who had ever met Beowulf knew that he would probably greet an armed robber with his usual sloppy enthusiasm. But when the laughter stopped, both of Audrey's parents were still doubtful. But then Audrey said, "I was thinking I might call Lizzie and see if she could come over."

That helped. "Oh, that would be nice," Audrey's mom said. "You might even ask her to have lunch with you. There's plenty of tuna for sandwiches."

Hannah Abbott hadn't yet met Lizzie, but she'd heard a lot about her from both Audrey and John. Particularly from John, who was still raving about Lizzie and her amazing artistic talent.

And what Audrey said about calling Lizzie wasn't really a lie. Not exactly. She *was* thinking about it. After she did her little experiment with the pen, which was almost certain not to take very long, or lead to anything, she *would* call, and who knows? Maybe Lizzie would be able to come over.

So after John Abbott very slowly and carefully wheeled himself out the door and down to Hannah's beat-up old Toyota, Audrey closed and locked the front door, then stood for a moment with her back against it, looking and listening.

The house was very quiet and empty. Beowulf, as soon as he had finished seeing John and Hannah off, had gone back to collapse on his pad, and no cockatiel sounds of any sort were coming from the kitchen. Taking a deep breath, Audrey headed for her room.

Once there, she immediately went to the window and, pushing the curtains aside, looked out toward the hill. Toward the steep hillside that rose up in a series of terraces behind the house to where, just beyond the highest terrace, the secret path began. From there, it wound its way up through groves of bay and oak trees and across slippery barren slopes to the bottom of an even steeper cliff. A cliff overgrown with vines and, behind the curtain of vines, the cave. Going back to her desk, Audrey sat down, pulled out the bronze pen and her secret novel notebook, and opened to the page where she had started to write about going to the cave.

For the next several seconds she stared at the words she had written and asked herself what she was planning to do and what she thought it might accomplish. What she had already written was:

The Cave
I want to go

She stared at the smooth, darkly flowing letters for a long time before she began to flip back through the pages, stopping to look for all the other places where she had used the pen.

But the first time, when she had been writing to warn the old woman about the police, she had been writing in her school binder—if she had written at all. When she'd looked afterward she hadn't been able to find it. Somehow she had managed to lose it, or else she'd only thought about writing it and never really did. So that didn't prove anything, one way or another.

The next time she'd used the pen she had written in her novel notebook when she was still working on her story about the girl detective. She flipped through the pages until she came to the one titled:

Heather's Alley Adventure

And then . . . Audrey paused, nodding thoughtfully. It had been that very night that Beowulf, and Sputnik, too, had begun to talk. They had talked, and then they had stopped talking. It was important to remember that she hadn't written that she herself, Audrey Abbott, could talk to animals, or even that she wanted to. So being able to talk to animals wasn't something she'd asked for. Not exactly.

Next came the page where she had started the picture book for young readers. The only entry there was the title written in pencil:

Debby's Dragon

But after that, when she wrote the short story about the baby dragon in the little picture book, she *had* used the pen, of course. And it had been that night when she'd seen, or dreamt she'd seen, the dragon.

It was a fascinating thing to think about. But it didn't seem to prove that if she wrote something with the pen, it would come true. It was more as if when she wrote about something, maybe some part of what she had written would happen, but not necessarily what you might expect.

It was a very exciting idea, but also very confusing. After some more thought she decided that the safest thing might be to begin by writing about the cave itself as it actually existed before she went on to try to put the rest of it into words—the part about the old woman and what she had, or had not, said and done.

So she would start with a kind of history of how she happened to know about the cave. And then she'd hope that whatever might follow would be like the newest chapter to the story that might be called *Audrey and the Cave on Wild Oaks Hill*. A chapter that might possibly include a duck, some owls, and a strange, shadowy creature who knew what you were thinking and probably knew exactly what might happen when you wrote with a magic pen and how you might be able to control it.

Turning to the next blank page and picking up the bronze pen, Audrey began to write:

THE CAVE ON WILD OAKS HILL

The cave is formed by a deep crack in a vine-covered hillside at the end of a steep, slippery path. The first time I went there, I was only five years old, but it wasn't exactly my idea. I was playing on our high terrace when Patricia Mayberry went by carrying some ragged blankets in a big wooden box. When I asked her where she was going, she said, "I'm going to a very mysterious place. You want to come?" And when I said I did, she showed me the trail to the cave. I must have taken a long time to get there that first day because it was a hard climb for a five-year-old, and on the way Patricia told me about the pretend game about pirates that she and her brother James had been playing.

When we finally got there, James was angry when he saw me because he said I would tell. But when I crossed my heart and promised that I never would, he said all right, I could play.

Everybody knew the twins played lots of pretend games, but they never had asked me to play before. So when they started letting me be a part of the pirate game, I was really excited.

She could remember it so clearly. Thinking back over what had happened and how she had felt about it made it seem so close and real. James, who read many books about pirates, was the one who contributed most of the important facts. Things like which of the pirates was the most famous and all the awful things they did to their victims. He and Patricia had even made pirate costumes. She could picture the whole scene so clearly. The twins in their pirate costumes—bandanas around their heads and skulls and crossbones skillfully drawn in black crayon on the chests of their T-shirts. And she could also see the pirate furniture that the twins had made themselves— the old splintery table and the chairs made of wooden crates.

Blinking her eyes to shut out the distracting pictures, she went on writing.

> My favorite part of the game was when we played we were the pirates named Blackbeard and Morgan and Bartholomew. James always got to be Blackbeard because he'd made himself a curly black beard out of some hair he'd swept up in his mother's beauty shop. Patricia and I took turns being the other two: Morgan the Terrible and Bartholomew the Elegant.
>
> But sometimes we were the pirates' victims. People who had been captured and were

prisoners in the cave while they waited to be murdered if they didn't get ransomed. I liked that part of the game too, at least I did when it didn't get too scary, like one time when

She stopped writing then. She could bring back exactly how it had been to be a pirates' victim. Putting the pen down on the notebook, she closed her eyes and reached back in her memory, remembering exactly what it was like to sit on one of the boxes playing the part of a prisoner. Her legs had been too short for her feet to touch the ground, and the rough wood of the box scratched the backs of her legs. And her wrists had been tied tightly behind her.

And then suddenly, so suddenly that she could do nothing to stop it from happening, they really were. There had been the briefest moment of some kind of movement, a feeling of lifting and floating, and then her wrists really were tied behind her back, her eyes were blindfolded, and the air was full of the damp, musty scent of the cave.

CHAPTER 16

AUDREY SQUIRMED, TWISTING HER HANDS
so hard that the rope scratched her wrists painfully. She tried again, pulling and twisting even harder,
but still without the least success. There had been a time,
she couldn't help remembering, when she and the twins
were being pirate victims and James Mayberry had tied
her up too tightly, making her angry and a little bit frightened. She'd told them so.

"Okay, you guys," she'd said to the twins. "Untie me
right now. I don't want to play anymore." Then Patricia
told James to say he was sorry and untie the rope, and he
did. But this time when Audrey said it again, just the way
she had before—"Untie me right now. I don't want to play
anymore."—there was no answer. No answer and no sound
at all.

When she blinked her eyes, she could feel her eyelashes
brushing against the heavy material of the blindfold, but

she couldn't see even the smallest glint of light. Except for the scratchy pain around her wrists and the familiar earthy scent of the cave, there was nothing her senses could tell her about where she was and what was happening.

After a while she stopped struggling and sat still, trying to clear her mind so that she could think more rationally. There had to be some kind of an explanation as to what was happening, if only she could calm down and concentrate. She had been in her own room, writing at her desk, and then, without any warning, she was tied and blindfolded and perhaps, judging by the smell, back in the pirate cave. The one thing she felt quite certain of was that this time there was no chance that this was just a dream. No dream could be so real and immediate, with no hint of any way to stop or rethink it. She was definitely and completely tied up and blindfolded, and there was no way to find out how or why it had happened or who had done it. Where was she? Was anyone else there?

She wanted to ask aloud. To call out, *Who did this? Who tied me up? Is somebody there?* She took a deep breath and opened her mouth, but she couldn't make the words come out. Either her vocal cords had been paralyzed by fright or she had forgotten how to speak.

But she could still listen. Holding her breath to silence even the sound of air moving through her nose and mouth, she strained her ears, but there was nothing to hear. Nothing except . . .

It was very faint at first, but then, gradually, it began to be a little more clear. She was hearing voices. The sound of one voice and then others. Not the voices of the Mayberry twins. Not at all. What Audrey seemed to be hearing now was quite different. Men's voices, deeper and older. Speaking in some other language. Definitely not English and not any language that sounded at all familiar.

The voices went on. The deepest, gruffest one, followed by others. One talking and then another answering. And then two of them talking at once, angrily. Perhaps arguing about her? About what to do with her?

What was it that James used to say about the kinds of things the pirates did to their captives? She could bring to mind easily enough, if she wanted to, distinct memories of James's stories about walking the plank and terrible beatings with whips called cat-o'-nine-tails.

The voices grew louder and then faded, and other sounds started—heavy thuds like axes chopping and the raspy slish-slash of a saw. And then, after another spell of silence, there was the smell of smoke—the woodsy, spicy smoke of a bonfire. And the angry voices again.

James had never said that pirates were cannibals, but for some obscure reason the fire was the last straw to complete a convulsion of absolute terror. All at once Audrey was struggling violently, pulling with all her strength at the ropes that bound her wrists and scooting forward on the box on which she was sitting. Wiggling forward until the box tipped and she fell, landing with a painful thud on her side and right arm. A thud, a sharp pain, and then silence. Silence but no longer complete blindness.

It seemed that the fall had partly dislodged the blindfold, and Audrey now found that she was able to see. Still lying helplessly on her side, she could see at least dimly with one partly uncovered eye. And what she saw was . . . Pirates? Three shadowy figures were moving slowly toward her. Vague, unrecognizable figures, only dimly seen, except that the nearest one's narrow face was almost completely covered by a thick black beard.

She was starting to scream, opening her mouth and taking a deep breath, when suddenly the silence was broken by other noises. A flowing river of sound, like wind-ruffled leaves or feathers. With her one uncovered eye, Audrey could see only a dense feathery cloud. A moment later something was touching the ropes that bound her wrists, and then they were free. Her hands were free, the blindfold was gone, and she was flying through the air. Moving easily and swiftly, with no effort at all on her part, she felt herself surrounded and lifted up by a rushing, whispering cloud of wings. A cloud so dense that its feathery touch forced her to close her eyes as she was carried higher and higher and then began to glide downward until she was gently deposited on . . .

Audrey blinked her eyes, looked around, and realized

that she was sitting on the floor of her own room. As she started to struggle to her feet, she was once again aware of a last feathery rush of air and a high, creaky voice saying, "Wisely, my dear. And to good purpose."

Standing now, Audrey turned slowly in a circle. No one was there and nothing had changed. On her desk was the notebook in which she had been writing, and there, on top of the page, was the bronze pen. She picked up the pen and held it briefly before quickly putting it down and going to the window. Nothing there. Nothing out of the ordinary. Only the terraced hillside and, farther up, the sun, still high in the midday sky.

It couldn't be true, could it? She couldn't have been transported to the cave and back again. And in between she hadn't been tied and blindfolded while some unknown people nearby talked in a strange foreign language, right? Turning away, she went to the mirror above her dresser and stared long and hard at her own face. It looked normal. No sign of a blindfold. Her pale brown hair was a tousled mess, but it often was, so that didn't prove anything.

She had gone back to her desk and was starting to pick up the pen when she suddenly noticed something that made her catch her breath in a sharp gasp. Right there, clearly visible around both of her wrists, were circles of rough, reddened skin. And that wasn't all. On her right arm, halfway between the shoulder and elbow, there was a large red scratch. A scratch that definitely hadn't been there until . . . until, struggling to free her hands, she had fallen painfully on her right side. Still rubbing the tender place on her arm, Audrey sat down at her desk and reached out slowly and uncertainly to pick up the bronze pen.

CHAPTER 17

As she reached for the pen, Audrey was not intending to write anything. In fact, at that particular moment she was seriously thinking she might never write with it again. She was only feeling a need to hold it, as if just the touch of it on her fingers might somehow help her to learn its secret. But now, holding it gingerly in both hands and thinking back over the recent past, she began to feel, or imagine she was feeling, a living thing. A thing that didn't move so much as quiver, or perhaps tingle with a kind of deep inner force.

Suddenly opening her desk and shoving the pen inside, Audrey quickly and firmly closed the drawer, and then sat still, staring into space. Staring, but not really thinking, at least not in any very productive way, until the door to her room suddenly opened. Audrey whirled around to see that it was only Beowulf.

What a relief! Throwing her arms around his warm,

doggy-smelling body, Audrey wrestled him to the floor. It was a few minutes later, while she was still lying with her cheek on Beowulf's well-padded rib cage, that she remembered that she had promised to call Lizzie. To call and ask Lizzie Morales if she wanted to come over and keep her company while her parents were in town.

On her way to the telephone in the kitchen Audrey was thinking Lizzie probably wouldn't come. After all, it was Saturday and it was quite likely that she'd already made other plans. Or maybe she'd be too busy working on one of her caricatures. Audrey sighed, thinking about all the things John Abbott had said about Lizzie's caricatures. Things like "amazingly original" and "surprisingly sophisticated."

She sighed again, wondering if her dad would think any of her stories were all that original or sophisticated—that is, if she ever decided to let him read them. As she dialed, she was still wondering what he might say.

But then the phone was answered by one of Lizzie's brothers, who yelled, "Hey, Liz! It's for you," so loudly that it jarred everything else right out of Audrey's head, at least for the moment. By the time she said, "Hi, Lizzie. Could you come over today?" she was simply hoping the answer would be yes. And it was.

"I'll be there in fifteen minutes," Lizzie said. And when Audrey told her she didn't think that was possible, Lizzie said, "Maybe not by bus, but I think it will be about that

long by Harley-Davidson. I'll be coming by motorcycle."
When Audrey asked what on earth she was talking about,
Lizzie explained that one of her brothers had one. "Mario
has a new motorcycle, and I just happen to have something
on Mario," she whispered. "Something I'll promise to be
very quiet about, if he'll just give me a ride now and then
when I really need one."

The threat must have worked because Audrey barely
had time to change into a long-sleeved shirt to hide her
wounded wrists before a motorcycle roared to a stop in
front of the Abbott house. A few seconds later there was a
knock on the door.

The first thing they did after Lizzie's arrival—that is,
the first thing after Lizzie bounced around Beowulf on
all fours, copying his usual welcoming ceremony—was to
have lunch. When Audrey asked Lizzie if she'd like to eat,
Lizzie said, "Would I! What a great idea. I'm starving."

Audrey wanted to ask why she was starving, but she
couldn't think of a polite way to do it. For instance, you
couldn't just ask somebody if her family was too poor
to buy enough food. But then, as if she were reading
Audrey's mind, Lizzie said, "On Saturday mornings any-
body with five brothers has to move fast or starve, and
today I overslept." She grinned at Audrey. "So, what are
we having?"

While they were eating the tuna sandwiches, they
talked mostly about their families. A little about Audrey's

parents, where they were and why, but mostly about Lizzie's family. Which was fine with Audrey. Lizzie's crazy stories about her brothers were almost interesting enough to keep Audrey's mind off the bronze pen and what it might, or might not, have caused to happen.

Lizzie had just finished telling Audrey about how Juan, her youngest brother, had been caught borrowing other people's clothes without permission and had been sentenced to doing the laundry for a whole week. To get even, he'd tied dozens of dripping-wet socks into extremely tight knots so that when they'd been through the dryer, they were stiff as cement. And then Alberto got even by throwing all of Juan's shoes up on top of the roof. Lizzie had gotten about that far when suddenly, without meaning to or thinking ahead, Audrey found herself saying, "I could use that. In a funny story, I mean. Okay?"

"For a story?" Lizzie asked. "Do you write stories?" She grinned and nodded. "Oh, sure, you wrote that dragon thing for little kids. But I mean, do you do other stuff?" And then, not even waiting for Audrey to answer, she went on, "Sure you do! I should have guessed."

It took a moment for Audrey to stop biting her tongue, but then, under the influence of Lizzie's obvious enthusiasm, she confessed. "Yes. I write. I've been doing it most of my life, but I usually don't like to talk about it."

"Oh yeah? Why not?"

Audrey sighed. Sighed again, then shrugged. "I

don't know. Except that most people think it's kind of a stupid thing to plan on. You know. Like planning to be Miss America or a famous movie star, or like that."

Lizzie nodded thoughtfully. "No," she said. "It's not like that. At least it's not if you do it because—because it's just what you do. Like drawing is just what I do."

Audrey nodded—slowly. She liked the part about it being just what you do. That part was true. But the other part was *why*. Why was it "just what you do?" She was wondering if drawing was what Lizzie did because it got her a lot of praise and attention. "Would you go on drawing if—," she began, but Lizzie got there ahead of her.

"You mean, would I draw if no one ever saw what I did, or if they saw it and thought it was the pits?" She paused, and then before Audrey could answer, she went on. "Sure I would. I would if *I* liked it. Do *you* like what you write?"

Audrey was saying, "Yes, I do. Mostly I do . . ." when Lizzie pushed back her chair and stood up.

"Okay. Let's see it."

Audrey sat still. "See what?" she said. "What do you mean?"

"I mean I want to see some of your stuff," Lizzie said.

On their way down the hall, with Beowulf padding along behind them, Audrey was still shaking her head and wondering why she was doing this. She went on shaking her head internally while she took the novel notebook out of its hiding place, at the same time wondering if she hadn't been unconsciously hoping this would happen when she'd asked Lizzie if she could use her brothers' socks in a story someday.

CHAPTER 18

AS LIZZIE SAT DOWN AT THE DESK AND started leafing through the secret notebook, Audrey suddenly reached over and slammed it shut.

"Why?" Lizzie said.

"You have to promise me something first."

"Okay. Like what?" Lizzie asked.

"That you won't tell anyone. That you won't tell my parents or anyone at school about my writing."

Lizzie grinned. "Well, sure," she said. "I promise. See, I'm raising my right hand and swearing." She leaned over and grabbed one of Beowulf's paws and held it up. "See? Beowulf is swearing too, aren't you, you great big gorgeous thing?"

Beowulf looked so pleased with himself, wagging his tail and grinning, that for a moment Audrey thought of telling Lizzie about the time he'd actually said a few things. But she didn't. Instead, she quickly turned away and went over to sit on the bed while Lizzie took her time turning the pages of the notebook, stopping to make comments every few minutes. Comments like, "Hey, I like this about the weird sneaky things the gorgeous flower does to people." And a little later, "I like the dog telling on the sneaky cat. Funneee stuff!" She was still reading the last few pages of the mystery about the girl detective who could talk to animals when there was the sound of a car in the driveway.

With the novel notebook safely back in its hiding place, Audrey and Lizzie were waiting at the front door when Audrey's parents came in. John Abbott introduced Lizzie to Hannah before he headed for his room to rest, and the other three went to the kitchen for apple juice and cookies.

Lizzie and Hannah got along fine. Audrey had been pretty sure they would, but you never knew these days with Hannah. Sometimes when she was extra tired or worried, she could find fault with almost anything or anyone. But today she was okay, and she laughed, almost out loud, when Audrey got Lizzie to tell her about Juan and the knotted socks.

So that was that. But before Lizzie headed for home, she said, "I'll be back next Saturday." And when Audrey said her dad's treatment was only every two weeks, so her folks would be at home, Lizzie said it didn't matter. "I won't tell them they have a talented author for a daughter, if that's what you're worrying about," she whispered.

So the week passed like all other weeks—at least like the weeks since Lizzie came to Greendale Junior High—with Audrey and Lizzie sitting together at lunch and during art class and getting lots of attention because everyone kept coming over to see what Lizzie was drawing.

And then it was Saturday again, and this time Lizzie arrived by bus, carrying her artwork briefcase. The first part of the visit was taken up by Lizzie showing Audrey's mom all the stuff she had already shown her father, and Hannah was almost as enthusiastic as John had been. And then when John Abbott went to his room to rest and Hannah went out to water the garden, Audrey and Lizzie went to Audrey's room.

This time they both sat on the floor. Lizzie returned to the story about the girl detective while Audrey once again went through Lizzie's briefcase. It was the first time she had been able to look at the pictures by herself with no one else there to interrupt her reactions. Except that every once in a while Lizzie stopped long enough to make comments about what she had just read.

At one point Lizzie said, "Hey, this part is great," and when Audrey went over to see what she was talking about, she saw that Lizzie was reading the page where she'd used the bronze pen to write about the girl detective and the talking animals.

"What part do you mean?" she asked. "The story or the handwriting?"

Lizzie laughed and said, "Both. Writing with that pen makes your handwriting a lot easier to read, that's for sure, but what I meant was, right here the whole story starts to make you feel like you can't wait to see where it's going. Particularly when the animals start talking. You know what I mean?"

"Yes," Audrey agreed. "I guess I do. I guess the part about the animals turned out to be very . . ."

She paused and Lizzie said, "Turned out to be what?"

But Audrey only shrugged and said, "The most important part, I guess," and went back to looking through the caricatures of famous people.

When Lizzie got to the place in the notebook where the title of the picture book was written in pencil at the top of one page, she said, "Hey, here's our story." She flipped to the next page and back again. "Where's the rest of it?"

Audrey explained how she'd written the rest of *Debby's Dragon* in the little booklet she'd made. And once again she thought about saying more. About telling Lizzie something about how she herself, as a little kid, had a pretend baby dragon. And then possibly go on to tell her what happened that night after she'd written the dragon story.

She didn't, though. Actually, one reason she didn't was because Lizzie had started to rave about how their book was such a fantastic primary-grade story and how everybody who saw it thought it was good enough to be published. "It really is a neat story," she said, and then grinned and added, "And the illustrations aren't bad either."

Next came the long essay Audrey had started writing just last Saturday about the cave and the pirates. Not fiction this time. Just a careful account of what the cave was like and what she had done there. Audrey watched as Lizzie read it through carefully and then turned back and read it again. After the second time she sat there staring at the page for a while before she looked at Audrey and said, "This is all true, isn't it? There really is a cave. And the part about the pirate game—that's true too."

Audrey found herself nodding.

"These twins . . ." Lizzie glanced down at the page. "These Mayberrys. They were, like, real people?"

"They still are," Audrey said. "Only they live in Arizona now. They used to live up the street. Number one twenty-four, where the Feltons live now."

"Wow," Lizzie said. "So the Mayberrys moved away, and that was the end of the game. No more pirates, huh? Too bad." She thought for a minute, nodding her head and squinting her eyes, before she said, "What happened then? I mean, you stopped right here where you're saying something about one time when it got too scary."

Too scary? Audrey caught her breath—and then laughed. "Oh, that. I was just going to write about when we were being the pirates' victims and James Mayberry tied me up so tight that it hurt, and it scared me. But he untied me when Patricia told him to."

Lizzie nodded. "And so that was all there was to it?"

"Well . . ." Audrey turned her eyes away from Lizzie's eager gaze before she shrugged and said, "Yes, that was all."

Lizzie's slow nod and curled lower lip might have been saying she didn't believe it. After a long pause she went on, "I want to see it. The cave. Right now. Okay?"

Audrey started to argue. She started by saying that she'd promised not to go there again, but that didn't help at all. In fact, it just seemed to make Lizzie even more determined. "Oh yeah?" she said. "Why? Why did you have to promise that?" And before Audrey had time to even think about how to answer, Lizzie asked, "Couldn't we just go for a walk and wind up going there?" She was grinning. "You know. Kinda by accident?"

"I don't think so," Audrey said. "It takes almost half an hour just to get there, even if you're a good climber. And almost as long to come back. No. We'd have to be gone too long, unless . . ." Audrey paused, thinking. Thinking about an intriguing possibility.

"Unless what?" Lizzie urged. "Tell me. Unless what?"

Audrey blinked, shook her head, and then, moving as if in a trance, she picked up the notebook, went to her desk, opened the top drawer, and took out the bronze pen. Then she sat down and opened the notebook to a blank page. Lizzie was hanging over her, trying to see what she was doing.

"Hey, I get it," Lizzie said. "You're going to write that we want to go there. You're going to say something like, 'Lizzie Morales and I want to go to the cave.' Yeah! Write that."

The pen moved smoothly and easily across the page, so easily that it almost seemed to be moving under its own power while Audrey wrote:

> Lizzie Morales and I want to pay a very, very short visit to the cave on Wild Oaks Hill.

She stopped writing, put down the pen, and sat still, waiting to see if something, anything at all, would happen. Waited as a minute went by, and another minute, and two or three more.

Then Lizzie's hand was on her shoulder, shaking her and demanding, "Why isn't something happening? Who did you write that to?"

Grinning ruefully, Audrey said, "I don't know. Nobody, I guess. It was just a crazy idea."

For a while Lizzie went on staring first at Audrey, then at what she had written on the paper before she shrugged, grinned, and said, "Well, I guess whoever it was for didn't get the message. Don't worry about it. Nobody listens to me, either." She turned away and, after stooping to give Beowulf a quick pat, wandered over to the shelves and began to examine Audrey's dragon collection.

Afterward Audrey remembered that she was still sitting at her desk, looking at her notebook, when she was once again enclosed in, surrounded by, a dense cloud. A cloud that brushed feathery fingers across her face and arms, forcing her eyes to close and filling her ears with a chorus of chirping, twittering sounds. The cloud lifted her up and away and then, very quickly, put her down on solid ground. On solid ground that she recognized, as soon she was able to open her eyes, as the rocky floor of the Wild Oaks cave.

Audrey jumped to her feet instantly, her eyes darting fearfully out toward the place just beyond the entrance, where the pirates had appeared. No pirates. Only a busy fluttering of small blackbirds, in and out of the dangling curtain of vine. Greatly relieved, she turned back to see another familiar sight. A row of owlish eyes were staring down at her from the far wall. And up above? Yes, the bats were there too, just as before, forming a lumpy, squeaky carpet across the roof of the cave. In the dim light it was hard to tell if there was anything way back on the ledge except the lumpy pile of rugs and blankets. But suddenly something was there. Emerging from the darkness at the back of the cave, it moved forward until . . . until Audrey was able to see that it was only the white duck.

As the duck moved closer, Audrey squatted down and, holding out her hand, whispered, "Hello, duck." And, just as before, its dignified waddle continued until its beak rested in Audrey hand. And that was all, except just as the wide, warm beak touched her hand, a voice that seemed to come from nowhere and everywhere whispered, "Wisely and to good purpose, my dear." At almost the same instant Audrey was once again caught up in the feathery cloud, floated up and up, and deposited . . . back into the chair in her own room. Back at her desk just as the door opened and Lizzie appeared looking startled and upset, saying, "There you are. Where did you go?"

CHAPTER 19

AUDREY AND LIZZIE STARED AT EACH other silently for a few seconds before they both began to talk at once.

"Wha-what happened?" Audrey stammered. "I mean, did you see anything?"

"Where have you been? What do you mean, did I see anything?" Lizzie demanded. "I didn't see anything, except I was over there looking at your dragons, and when I turned around, you were gone. I looked in the closet and under the bed and everywhere, and then I went down the hall and looked in the living room and kitchen. But no one was there, either. Your mother is still out in the garden and your dad is in his room, but you weren't anywhere. But then I came back here—and you're here again." Putting her hands on her hips, Lizzie demanded, "So tell me. Where did you go?"

For a long moment Audrey stared at Lizzie before she said, "You aren't going to believe me but . . ."

"Try me," Lizzie said.

So she did. "I think it's like this," Audrey said. "Sometimes what I write with this pen comes true, but just kind of. I mean, when I started to use it to work on the story about the girl detective, you know, the part where the animals were talking, it happened. Beowulf—and Sputnik, too—started talking to me. They really did—in actual words."

"Yeah?" Lizzie looked delighted. "What did old Beowulf say?"

Audrey couldn't help smiling. "Well, when I poked him with my toe, he told me that people shouldn't kick their dogs."

Lizzie looked at Beowulf. "Right on, monster dog," she said. "You are *so* right." Beowulf opened one eye, waved his tail, and went back to sleep.

"But it didn't last long," Audrey went on. "Only about one day and then it was over. But right after I wrote the dragon book, that same night there was . . ." She stopped and took a deep breath before she went on. "That night there *was* a dragon under my bed. It's true. I know you don't believe me, but it is true."

"Yeah?" Lizzie said. Getting down on her hands and knees, she looked under the bed and went on looking for a minute or two. When she finally got up, she was grinning. "Well, there's no dragon there now, but one was there not long ago."

"What do you mean?" Audrey was amazed. "How can you tell?"

Lizzie shrugged and grinned. "I don't exactly know. Maybe it's the smell." Her grin widened. "People who know as much about dragons as I do can usually sniff them out." She paused, looking from Audrey to the notebook on her desk and back again. "So you're telling me that after you wrote that, you . . ."

Audrey nodded. "It worked," she said. "It happened. That's where I was just a minute ago."

When she raised her eyes, she saw that Lizzie was returning her stare and nodding slowly. Nodding and frowning, nodding and frowning. But when she finally began to talk, what she said was, "Yeah, but what I don't understand is why I didn't get to go too." She pointed to the notebook. "You wrote that we both wanted to go." She stared and Audrey stared back.

"I know. It doesn't make any sense. But none of it does."

"Yeah, I know." Lizzie's frown faded. "But what's wrong with that? Who said everything has to make sense?" She picked up the notebook and, sitting down on the bed, motioned for Audrey to sit beside her. "Now start at the beginning and tell me about how you got this pen and what happened every time you used it. Okay?"

Audrey sat down, but at first she didn't have much to say. "No, I don't think . . ." A long pause. "Well, maybe I could just . . ." Another pause before she said, "It didn't start out with the pen. That happened later."

"Okay. Okay, what *did* it start with?"

Somehow that was what did it. If Lizzie hadn't asked that exact question at that particular moment, it was quite likely that Audrey never would have gotten around to telling her the whole story. But when Lizzie said "what *did* it start with," it was just too much of a temptation to say, "A duck. It all started with a white duck." To say just that much, then sit back and watch the expression on Lizzie's face.

Expressions (plural), actually, because Lizzie's went from amazement to suspicion (as in: *Stop kidding me*) to worry (as in: *Are you feeling all right?*). So Audrey had a lot of explaining to do. Starting with, "It's true." Then she went on to, "I'm not kidding." And then, "And I'm not crazy, either."

Stopping long enough to take a deep breath, she said, "It all began about a month ago when I was sort of hiding out on the highest terrace behind our house, and all of a sudden there was a big white duck, right behind me on the path. It came right up to me until I touched it, and then it went back the way it had come, looking back, as if it had come to get me and was waiting for me to follow it."

Audrey went on, telling about how she had almost seen, more like sensed, really, someone, perhaps an old woman, in the cave and how she had gone back a second time. And then after she asked if she could do something to help, like bring food or blankets, the woman gave her the pen. And after that how she had stupidly told her parents about seeing the woman, and they decided she was only a poor old bag lady who needed to be put in an institution and insisted they had to tell the police.

"That was the first time I wrote with the pen," she told Lizzie. "I wrote that I wanted to warn her about the police. I wanted to send the note or take it to her, but I didn't think I could. But when I looked for it later, it was gone. I thought I must have lost it or else only imagined writing it in the first place. But maybe . . ." She stopped, considering for the first time another explanation of what might have happened: Maybe because she *had* written that she wanted to *send* a warning, the warning *had* been sent?

"So when the police got there?" Lizzie said, making it into a question.

Audrey nodded. "She wasn't there."

"Because she got your warning?" Lizzie asked.

"Maybe. Anyway, the police didn't find anything, so my folks thought I'd lied about the woman or else . . ."

"Or else what?" Lizzie demanded.

"Or else I'd just imagined her." She shrugged ruefully. "I guess they think that I'm either a liar or a little bit nuts."

Lizzie only nodded thoughtfully, chewing on her lower lip, so Audrey went on, "And after that there was the time when I'd been writing about talking animals and—"

"Oh, yes." Lizzie interrupted. "And old Beowulf told you off for kicking him. And Sputnik got his two cents in too."

"Yes, and then there was the dragon-under-the-bed story."

"Yeah," Lizzie said thoughtfully. "I want to hear more about that one. But when you wrote that long thing about the pirate game in the cave with the twins and all that stuff? Did anything happen to you after you wrote that one?"

Audrey thought for a moment, once again wondering how much she should tell. The pirates would be hard to describe and a lot harder for anyone, even Lizzie, to believe. But finally she took a deep breath and began. "Well, I wrote that page last Saturday before I called and asked you if you wanted to come over. My folks had just left to see my dad's doctor when I wrote about the cave and the pirates." Another long pause. "And then I was there."

She went on, talking faster and faster, her words stumbling over each other. "Only, I was blindfolded and my hands were tied behind my back so hard that my wrists really hurt, and I could hear voices talking in some foreign language, and I could smell smoke like from a campfire."

Audrey stopped and stared at Lizzie, and Lizzie stared back. "So that's what happened to your wrists," she said. "I wondered about that."

"You wondered about my wrists?" Audrey asked. "But I was wearing a shirt with long sleeves. How did you . . ."

"I know. On a hot day. I wondered about that. But then once when we were busy talking, you pushed your sleeves up, and I noticed. I was going to ask you what happened to them, but then I decided you'd tell me when you wanted to. So I didn't."

Lizzie hadn't asked, but she had seen the scratched places. Audrey held out her arms and twisted them from side to side. Even now, a week later, you could see a few reddish spots.

Lizzie was looking too. "Yeah," she said. "They're a lot better but you can still see it a little. See?" She grabbed Audrey's hand and turned it one way and then the other. "Right there, and there, too. Crummy pirates," she said.

It wasn't until then, when she said "crummy pirates," that Audrey really began to realize that Lizzie believed the whole story—pirates and all. And then she said something that made it even more certain. What Lizzie said was, "Okay. So now we need to decide what you could write with the pen so that whatever happens, it happens to both of us. Okay?"

It took Audrey a few seconds to understand that Lizzie actually meant it. But when she did, she felt she had to say, "But we already tried that, didn't we? I mean, when I wrote about both of us going to the cave, I was the only one who went while you were still here looking at the dragons. Maybe it's like the pen will only make things happen to me."

Lizzie looked disappointed. "You might be right." She thought for a minute before she went on. "Or else . . ." Lizzie's grin had a sneaky tilt to it. "Maybe it only works for whoever does the writing. Like, *you* wrote that we wanted to go to the cave, so *you* went. But maybe if *I'd* done the writing—" Lizzie acted it out, pretending to scribble with a nonexistent pen—"then I might have been the one to go. What do you think?"

For some reason Audrey had her doubts, but what she said was, "I guess that might be it. You could try it and see what happens."

"All *right!*" Lizzie said. Taking the notebook with her, she went to the desk, sat down, and picked up the bronze pen. Turning to the first blank page, she started to write.

CHAPTER 20

LOOKING OVER LIZZIE'S SHOULDER, Audrey watched as she wrote:

I want Beowulf to talk to me.
To ME, Lizzie Morales.

The script looked very similar to Lizzie's ordinary handwriting. A little darker perhaps, but not exactly the smooth, wide lines that seemed to flow almost automatically when Audrey held the bronze pen. But Lizzie didn't seem to notice the difference. As soon as she finished the sentence, she put the pen down decisively and, going over to where Beowulf was sleeping, sat down on the floor.

When Lizzie patted Beowulf on the head and said, "Hi there, you big beautiful monster," he opened one eye, gave his tail a limp wag, and went on with his nap. Lizzie looked up at Audrey, shrugged, patted Beowulf more firmly, said,

"Hi" again, and waited some more. Still no response. At last she got to her feet and gave him a firm poke with the toe of her shoe. That got some action. Beowulf opened both eyes and looked at Lizzie accusingly before he staggered to his feet, padded to the other side of the room, and collapsed again, quickly and firmly closing his eyes.

"Well, so much for that experiment," Lizzie said. "I guess that settles it. The pen just doesn't work for anyone but you."

"I guess maybe that's it," Audrey said. She nodded and then shook her head and then nodded it again before she said, "Or maybe you have to write a story about what you want to have happen. Like I did when I wrote about talking to animals. Maybe it didn't work for you because you only wrote a kind of wish."

Lizzie shook her head, slowly at first and then more decisively. "I don't think that's it. You wished you could send that warning, and it happened. And then you wished we could go to the cave, and you went, all right. But not me. So that's not it. Like I said, it just won't work for me."

They sat down again on the bed, and for a while neither one said anything. Lizzie stared off into space, and Audrey watched her cautiously, wondering what she was thinking.

Suddenly Lizzie said, "Okay. How about this? Maybe you write about something really out-of-this-world happening *right here* in the room. That way if I can't be a part of it, at least I can watch it happening."

That seemed like an interesting, if slightly alarming, possibility. "So, what kind of out-of-this-world thing should I have happen?" Audrey asked warily.

"Let's see." Lizzie looked around the room. "How about if you wrote . . ." After a moment she said, "I don't know. Maybe you could . . ." She got up then and walked around, stopping briefly to look at an old picture of Nellie Elgin, Audrey's grandmother, standing in front of the Elgin house when it was nice and new. Lizzie shook her head and went on to the dragon collection. When she picked up a particularly evil-looking purple dragon and examined it thoughtfully, Audrey quickly said she didn't think so.

Lizzie sighed, nodded, and, leaving the dragons, started on the books. She ran her fingers along the spines of the books, pausing now and then, but only briefly, until her hand stopped moving and she said, "Hey, *The Jungle Book*. That's one of my favorites. How about writing something about *The Jungle Book?*"

Audrey laughed. "Like what? Should I write about my room turning into a jungle?"

"Yeah," Lizzie said excitedly, and then she shook her head. "No. That might be too much to ask." She thought a bit longer before her eyes lit up again. "But maybe you could bring some of the characters from the book here?"

"Oh, sure." Audrey's smile was a little sarcastic. "Like the tiger or maybe the python? Right here in my bedroom?"

"Well, maybe not." After another long moment Lizzie rolled her eyes and grinned. "But you might ask for Mowgli?"

Audrey blinked, picturing a not-very-well-dressed jungle boy suddenly appearing in the middle of her room. It was a wild idea and she could imagine some problems that might arise, even if he only stayed for a minute. Like, for instance, how Beowulf might react. Of course the big dog always greeted strangers who came to the front door enthusiastically, but it was hard to say how he might feel about a stranger in a loincloth who arrived suddenly out of thin air.

Lizzie was saying, "Well, it may be a crazy idea, but it wouldn't hurt to try. I'll bet it could work." Audrey was weakening, actually beginning to accept the idea that a visit by Mowgli might be kind of exciting, when there was a loud rap on the door. Catching her breath in a sharp gasp, Audrey stared at the door. It opened—but it was just her mother.

"Oh, hi, Mom," Audrey said, trying not to sound as delighted as she felt. Well, pleasantly relieved, anyway. She must not have been entirely successful because Hannah Abbott looked surprised—and pleased.

"Hi, yourself," she said to Audrey, and then to Lizzie, "I've just discovered that I'm going to have to make a quick trip to the pharmacy. Would you like a ride home?" She looked at her watch. "It's getting late and the buses are pretty unreliable this time of day."

So Lizzie left, but before she went, she reminded Audrey that she wasn't going to be able to visit next Saturday because her whole family was leaving on a trip right after the last day of school.

"Oh yeah," Audrey said. "I almost forgot." She must have looked as disappointed as she felt because Lizzie said, "It's just for three weeks. And when I come back, it will still be summer vacation and we'll have lots of time to . . ." She paused and grinned as she went on, "To finish *The Jungle Book*."

As the two of them started out the door, Audrey heard her mother saying that she was glad to hear they were reading *The Jungle Book*, because it had been one of her favorites when she was young.

So then there was a week of school again—the last one before summer vacation. Most of the tests were over, but things were extra busy with practice sessions for the eighth-grade graduation ceremony, as well as the putting up of displays in every hall and classroom. Nearly one whole wall in the art room was hung with Lizzie's art, not only dragons and caricatures, but also things she'd done recently in art class, including the *Debby's Dragon* book, which was displayed in a very prominent spot. There was a lot to think about at school, but when Audrey was home, she was still spending a lot of time thinking about the bronze pen.

It wasn't until the first Monday of summer vacation that Audrey came up with an interesting theory. She was sitting at her desk at the time, holding the pen in her hand and looking at what Lizzie had written about talking to Beowulf. She asked herself for the umpteenth time why the pen had failed to do anything at all for Lizzie.

It was about then that she remembered reading somewhere that nothing would happen at séances or that sort of thing if someone who was a serious doubter was present. But that couldn't be the problem. If one thing was for sure and certain, it was that Lizzie really believed in the pen's power. Maybe even more than Audrey did.

But another explanation might be that Lizzie had failed because she had been too demanding—almost insisting that Beowulf talk to her! Maybe, *To* me, *Lizzie Morales* wasn't the kind of thing you should write with something like the bronze pen. After all, Audrey hadn't asked for *anything* when Beowulf and Sputnik started talking. She had simply written about a human being who could talk to animals. So perhaps it was all right to make a suggestion, but not to give an order.

That might be it. Probably not, but maybe it was worth a try. A test of some sort. Like, for instance, she might try giving an order. Try writing a demand for action of some sort and then, if nothing happened, try doing it again in a more polite, or at least indirect, way. Then, if the order didn't work and the request did, it would prove . . . what? Well, maybe that Lizzie ought to try again, only more politely this time. Not right away, of course, since she was away visiting relatives in Mexico, but maybe as soon as she got back.

So what should Audrey try demanding? Not something she really wanted a whole lot or needed badly, she decided. Just something she would like but could probably manage to do without, since this was the wish that wasn't at all likely to be granted. When nothing had come to mind after several minutes, Audrey got up and walked around the room, as Lizzie had done when she came up with the *Jungle Book* suggestion. Except that Audrey went right past the dragons and the bookshelves and the bed, coming to a stop in front of her chest of drawers. Pulling open one of the drawers, she stared inside briefly, then hurried back to sit at her desk and pick up the pen.

> I need

Remembering to be demanding, she crossed out the word "need" and put in "want":

> I ~~need~~ want a new two-piece bathing suit.
> Audrey Abbott.

No "please" and no "thank you." That ought to do it.

Sure enough, no bathing suit. Even after Audrey had waited patiently for nearly ten minutes and checked all the places it might be. Not on her desk and not on her bed and not in the drawer where she kept her old outgrown suit. So the next step would be to try it in a nicer way. Perhaps in a way that would be more like a mere suggestion. Or even a kind of story, like the ones about talking animals and the baby dragon. After some thought she began:

A girl named Audrey Abbott really wanted to go the Greendale Municipal Swimming Pool during her summer vacation. Her friend Lizzie said she would go too. Only there was just one problem. Audrey's bathing suit was a total loss. The thing was, Audrey was almost a teenager and she'd been growing a lot lately, especially in some places, and her old suit was definitely too small.

After reading over what she had written, Audrey went back and crossed out the word "small," and wrote "flat" instead.

Her old suit was definitely too ~~small~~ flat.

She thought briefly of adding something about how poor her family was now because of her dad's angina pectoris, but then she decided against it. A suggestion was one thing, but begging was another.

For the next five or ten minutes Audrey waited, sitting at her desk, before she got up and checked in all her dresser drawers and even in her closet. Not that she'd ever hung a bathing suit on a clothes hanger. But then again, maybe some people, or some magical forces, might. No bathing suit.

She sat on the edge of the bed and waited some more. She went on waiting as she stretched out on the bed and took a brief nap. When she woke up, she decided that there must be times when a suggestion, even if it's written as if it were part of a story, didn't work any better than just plain asking. And this must be one of them.

CHAPTER 21

OR AUDREY, ONE OF THE BEST THINGS about summer vacation had always been that she had more time to write. To write and, this summer at least, to spend a lot of time thinking about the bronze pen. Time to think and wonder why it had been given to her and what it really was.

That the pen had some sort of strange power, she really didn't doubt. Or, at least, she didn't doubt that it had right at first. Whether it was still able to do anything was another question, now that it had definitely failed the bathing suit tests. Both of them. She was dying to discuss the results of those tests with Lizzie, but since she was still in Mexico, that wasn't a possibility. So Audrey was left to wonder and worry by herself.

But she hated to give up and just accept that the pen was now only an ordinary writing tool. One that still seemed to write with an extra-broad, flowing line but, except for that, had no special power.

It was quite late one evening during that first week of summer vacation when she began to think of another test she might try. This time by writing one of the kind of things that had worked before. Something that had already caused something magical to happen. Like, for instance . . .

What about, once again, writing another story about the cave? She had actually picked the pen up and was even starting to think just how the story should go when her mind took her back to what it had been like to be tied up and blindfolded, listening to the harsh rasp of strange voices. Putting the pen down quickly and firmly, she thought some more.

Something about the baby dragon, perhaps? But then, remembering how large and vivid and startlingly real the dragon had been, she rather reluctantly thought not.

That left "Heather's Alley Adventure," which seemed to have caused Beowulf and Sputnik to become so talkative. That, she decided, was more like it. Flipping to the last page of the story she had written about the girl who could talk to animals, she once again picked up the pen.

Let's see. On the day when Beowulf and Sputnik started talking to her, she had just been writing about how the dog named Hero had talked to Heather and then to the cat with the evil yellow eyes. She read over the last page. The one she had written just a few minutes before she pushed Beowulf with her toe and found out not only that he could talk, but also that he disapproved of people kicking dogs.

The last paragraph she had written that night had ended:

> As the police ambulance pulled away from the curb, taking the murderer to the police station, Heather told the dog good-bye and thanked him once more for saving her life.
>
> "Good-bye, Hero," she told him. "Thanks again. It's been nice talking to you."

> THE END

So what should she write now? That particular story was pretty much finished. She sat with the pen poised over the page for several minutes while she tried to decide where the story should go from there.

She didn't really want to start a whole new adventure for Heather because that would involve setting the scene and finding a way to introduce the reader to the setting and characters, the way you always have to do when you start a new story. That would be too time-consuming. She simply wanted to write, as quickly as possible, about talking animals. As quickly as possible, she was thinking, when she suddenly came up with what seemed to be a good solution. In the pen's wide, flowing letters she wrote:

AFTERWORD
TO "HEATHER'S ALLEY ADVENTURE"

It wasn't until the police car had disappeared on its way to take the murderer to prison that Hero turned and went back down the alley to where he had talked to the cat with the yellow eyes. And there it was, still sitting on the tin roof of the shed, looking down at him with its strange yellow eyes.

"There you are," Hero said to the cat. "I want to talk to you."

The cat licked his paw and washed behind his left ear. "Why?" it said.

"Because I don't understand why you would try to help an evil murderer kill a very important person."

"What important person?" the cat asked.

"Heather," Hero said. "Heather is a very special person who can talk to animals, and besides that, she is my friend."

The cat washed his other ear thoughtfully before he said, "You are right. I was going to help the murderer because he gave me a can of tuna, and tuna is very important to me.

But I guess you are right. Friendship is more important than tuna."

"You are so right," Hero said. "Friendship is more important than anything. Let's shake on it."

So they did.

THE END

That ought to do it, Audrey thought, and looked around for Beowulf. He wasn't in his usual spot, sprawled out at the foot of her bed, so she went down the hall to the kitchen, but he wasn't there, either. She stopped for a moment by the birdcage, where Sputnik was sitting with his head tucked to one side in his nighttime pose. She came to a quick stop. Time for the first test.

"Hi, pretty bird," she whispered. "You want some more sunflower seeds?"

No answer. After she'd tried again with no result, she glanced at her watch. Ten thirty. Too late for a cockatiel to feel talkative? Maybe so. She went on into the living room, where Hannah Abbott was sitting on the saggy couch with her feet tucked under her, looking too small and thin to be the mother of an almost teenage daughter. Too small and thin—and, as usual, much too tired. No one else was there. No Beowulf.

"Where's Beowulf?" Audrey asked. "I was going to take him out, but he's not in my room."

"He's in your father's room," Hannah said. "He's taken to spending a lot of time in there in the evenings. Don't knock and wake your father. He's had such a hard time sleeping lately. Just open the door quietly and let Beowulf see you. He'll come."

Audrey nodded.

Beowulf was there, all right, sprawled out like a long-legged bear skin rug at the foot of her father's bed, and when Audrey opened the door, he lifted his head. Audrey opened the door wider and made a "come here" motion. Pausing only long enough to look in the direction of the bed where Audrey's dad was sleeping, Beowulf padded toward her.

It wasn't until they were on the back porch that Audrey grabbed his collar and pulled him to a stop. "Hey, Wulfy," she whispered. "How you doing?"

Beowulf wagged his tail. She tried again. Bending over with her mouth close to his floppy ear, she asked, "How come you didn't flake out in my room tonight? I missed you."

Beowulf wagged harder, licked Audrey's nose, pulled away, and trotted off to his favorite pooping spot. Wiping her nose with the back of her hand, Audrey sighed as she watched him go. It wasn't working. She had written about talking animals, and nothing of the sort had happened. So, she thought reluctantly, it was really true. The pen was no longer able to make anything happen, not even when you made up a story about what you wanted it to do.

She was still waiting by the back door when her mother went by, stopping to pat Audrey's shoulder and say good night. She had disappeared down the hall by the time Beowulf finally came back, so it was safe to make one last try.

"Hey, monster dog," Audrey said. "How come you're not speaking to me? Did I hurt your feelings?" No answer. Beowulf only trotted past her toward the living room. But then, just as he was passing Sputnik's cage, he suddenly slowed to a stop. Stopped dead still, in mid-trot, right beside the cage where the cockatiel was now awake and making a series of clucking, sputtering sounds.

Beowulf stopped and gazed toward the cage with his head tilted and his ears cocked, looking startled or at least surprised. Then he slowly moved closer. When his big fuzzy muzzle was almost touching the cage, he began to make a noise that Audrey had never heard him make before— not exactly a whimper, but not quite a growl, either. The clucking, sputtering, growling, whimpering noises went on for several minutes as Sputnik climbed down the side of his cage until his head was level with Beowulf's nose.

Audrey moved closer, but neither of them paid any attention to her. The funny noises went on for quite a while longer before Sputnik climbed back up to his usual perch, made one last loud cluck, flapped his wings, and went back to sleep. Beowulf went on watching the bird for a bit longer, with his head cocked first to one side and then to the other, before he trotted on into the living room and flopped down on his mattress.

Still feeling let down and depressed about the failure of her experiment, Audrey went to her room. It wasn't until the next day that she began to realize exactly what it was that she had witnessed in the kitchen that night.

CHAPTER 22

I T WAS LATE AFTERNOON OF THE FOLLOWING day, and Audrey was half watching a stupid show on the one snowy channel left on their ailing TV while her father was napping in his room when, right out of the blue, it suddenly hit her. *Maybe it had worked.* The bronze pen might have worked after all. Hurrying to her room, she got out her novel notebook and went over the pages she had written the night before—and, sure enough, she was right.

The thing was, in the new "Afterword" section she really *hadn't* gotten around to writing about a person talking to animals. Nothing at all about a human being talking to animals. What she had done was to write about animals talking to each other.

And now that she'd gotten that straight, she suddenly knew what Beowulf and Sputnik had been up to last night. What was probably happening when they were making all those funny noises at each other was a conversation. A two-way, dog-bird conversation.

Jumping up, she was on her way to test her theory when she realized it was probably too late. The other times the pen had caused something extraordinary to happen, it usually stopped happening fairly quickly—like, in just a few hours. But if she hurried, perhaps it wouldn't be entirely finished yet.

Once again she found Beowulf sleeping in her father's room. By opening the door and leaning forward, she was able to see her father's closed eyes and the silent rise and fall of his chest. She watched her father breathe—in and out, in and out—several times before she called Beowulf in an almost silent whisper. When Beowulf got to the door, she took his collar and quickly led him to the kitchen. But when they reached Sputnik's cage, nothing happened. At least nothing much. Just as he had before, the cockatiel did climb down from his high perch until he was on a level with Beowulf's nose, but neither of them said anything or even made any unusual sounds.

For a minute or two Audrey was hopeful as she watched Sputnik hang upside down on his cage wall, with his beak sticking out only a few inches from Beowulf's nose, but nothing else happened. Just as she had feared, it was too late. If they really had the ability to talk to each other last night, it obviously was all over now.

But as she stood there watching and hoping, it began

to be evident that there was a slight difference. The change was that, even though they weren't speaking, they did seem to be relating to each other in a more positive way. Had there really been a change, or was she just imagining it? How could she be sure?

Audrey glanced at her watch. Her mother wouldn't be home for a couple of hours, and her father seemed to be sleeping soundly. There ought to be time for Sputnik to do a little orbiting and relating to his favorite victim either in the same old way or, if her guess was right, in a new and more friendly manner.

"Listen, you crazy bird," Audrey whispered, "if I let you out of your cage, you have to promise to go back in when I tell you to. Okay?"

Of course he didn't promise, but Audrey imagined that his screech did sound a little bit more cooperative than usual. Anyway, she just had to find out, so she opened his door and let him fly.

As always, Sputnik started out by orbiting the living and dining rooms several times, swooping down close to her head and then to Beowulf's. No change there. But then she did begin to notice something new.

Today when he landed on Beowulf's head, instead of pecking, Sputnik put his beak down close to one of the big floppy ears and chirped at least once and maybe twice. More or less ordinary cockatiel-type chirps, only maybe a little softer than usual, and when Beowulf opened his eyes and raised his head, he didn't shake it or growl.

After that Sputnik orbited some more and, as usual, hung upside down from the chandelier. His squawks did seem to be in Beowulf's general direction, but somehow they sounded a little more like just showing off and a little less like a declaration of war. When it was time to put Sputnik back in his cage, he resisted like always and had to be threatened with the butterfly net before he gave up and went in. No change there.

By the time Hannah came home and dinner was over, Audrey had come to a firm decision—a fairly exciting one. The pen had worked after all. It *had* made something happen that she had just written about. The only problem was that what she had actually written about was animals talking to each other. So that was what she got.

And, just as before, it hadn't lasted very long. By the time she realized what had happened and let Sputnik out of his cage, it seemed to be mostly finished. Beowulf and Sputnik were no longer able to talk to each other. Not really talk, but there still did seem to be a slight improvement in the way they related to each other. So you might say that even though the spell was broken, something had definitely changed.

That wasn't hard to understand, Audrey decided. She was fairly sure that if you looked back through history, you'd discover that when people, even people from different countries, who spoke different languages found a way to talk to each other, they usually wound up being better friends. And there wasn't any reason to think the same thing wouldn't be true of Irish wolfhounds and cockatiels.

So what next? It still was quite a while before Lizzie would be back, but in the meantime, there ought to be something exciting that could be done with the pen, now that Audrey was certain, or fairly certain, that it was still working. But what should it be? One thing she did know was what it *shouldn't* be. Like writing about getting a new bathing suit, for instance. But why should that be true? Was it something about how and what she'd written? Or did the pen have something against bathing suits?

What was it the woman in the cave had said about writing? Oh, yes. Something about how she should write "wisely and to good purpose." Whatever that meant. Audrey was still wondering when she heard the wheelchair going down the hall. Her father was up and would be needing his afternoon medicine and cup of tea.

An hour or so later the two of them were reading in the living room when Mr. Potts, the mailman, came by and, as he often did, came in to see if everything was okay. Audrey appreciated Mr. Potts's frequent visits, even though they were a reminder that everyone, even the postman, knew her father was so sick that, at any time, Audrey might need help getting him to the emergency room at the hospital.

After he had checked to see if everything was all right,

Mr. Potts handed Audrey the mail, patted Beowulf, made his usual joke about how lucky he was that Beowulf wasn't a traditionalist about attacking mailmen, and went on down the road, just as usual. But there was something unusual in the stack of mail he left behind.

Along with the ordinary bills and advertisements, there was a letter for Audrey. A letter that had been mailed in Mexico City by Lizzie Morales. Audrey was pleased but more than a little surprised. She and Lizzie had talked about writing, but Lizzie had said she would be staying at different places with different friends and relatives every few days, so she couldn't leave a very reliable mailing address.

It had also occurred to Audrey that it might not be a good idea to write to Lizzie about anything very private— for instance, anything concerning the pen—because . . . well, because something might happen just like it was at that very moment. "A letter from Lizzie?" her father was saying. And even though he wasn't asking to read it, it was obvious that he was expecting Audrey to tell him what Lizzie had to say.

But Lizzie's letter didn't say anything that Audrey would mind letting her father see. She shouldn't have worried. Of course Lizzie, growing up with all those unpredictable siblings, would know better than to put anything really private in a letter. A letter that might be snatched out of her hands, or sidetracked on its way to the mailbox. In her letter Lizzie just told what she had been doing and seeing and some things about her Mexico City relatives. Nothing at all secret. The letter ended in an ordinary way by saying, *Wish you were here. Your friend, Lizzie.* And there was a return address, an address in Mexico City, on the envelope.

But now Audrey had another problem to solve. The problem of how to write to tell Lizzie about the latest thing that the pen's power had accomplished but say it in such a way that wouldn't be understood by anyone else who might get their hands on it. It wasn't going to be an easy thing to do.

It was a situation in which a secret code would be very useful. Audrey wished she and Lizzie had thought to invent one before the Moraleses left. But they hadn't, so that was that. So how could she let Lizzie know the latest news about the pen? It wasn't until late that evening that Audrey came up with an interesting possibility. Hurrying to her room, she got out her box of stationery, took out the bronze pen, and began to write.

CHAPTER 23

Hello Lizzie,

As you see, I'm writing to you with my special pen.

From there, the letter went on in a very ordinary way. The way anyone would answer a letter from a friend who was away on a trip.

I was really happy to get your letter. It sounds like you are having an awesome time and I wish

Oops! It might not be a good idea to write, *I wish I could be there too*, because if she did, she just might be. Might appear suddenly in the middle of a lot of aston-ished Moraleses, without any possible way to explain how she got there. So . . . how to go on? After some thought she continued that particular sentence:

I wish that, someday <u>in the future</u>, I might get to see Mexico City.

So far so good, except that she still hadn't said anything to let Lizzie know about the bathing suit test and, even more important, what had happened when she wrote about animals talking to each other. It really seemed important to let Lizzie know. What could she say that Lizzie would understand but nobody else would? Maybe something like:

Oh, yes. You know those tests we were working on? I've been doing some experiments, and I think that it really does work the way you thought it did. It sort of does, anyway, if you do it in just the right way. Let's work on it some more when you get back. Okay?

See you soon.

Sincerely,
Your friend,
AUDREY

There. Audrey felt sure Lizzie would know what that meant. Putting the letter in an envelope, she sealed it securely. And tomorrow, after she'd asked Mr. Potts how much postage would be necessary to send a letter to Mexico, she would get it in the mail. And in two weeks, when Lizzie returned, they would think of some new ways to prove that writing with the pen would make whatever you wrote about—or at least a part of what you wrote about—come true.

So the letter went off with Mr. Potts the next day, and Audrey went back to worrying and wondering. Wondering about the pen and worrying about her father's sick heart.

And then, only a few days later, there was more to worry about. Her mother came home from work that evening feeling even worse than usual. Some things hadn't gone well at the office, and Mrs. Austin had been even meaner and more critical than usual. Audrey's mother had come home bringing some Chinese takeout food because, as she told Audrey, she was feeling too depressed to even think about cooking. She even cried a little while they were dishing out the chop suey and chow mein, with big tears rolling down her cheeks and clumping the long lashes on her famous eyes. But by the time Audrey's father came to the table, she had dried her tears and stopped talking about the terrible things Mrs. Austin had said and done. Stopped entirely, with not a word about her terrible day during dinner. Not even one.

Audrey went to her room that night feeling concerned about her mother but even more worried about her father. She was almost sure that the reason her mother had stopped complaining, which she hardly ever did, must be because John's heart was worse. So much worse that it would dangerous to say or do anything that might upset him in any way.

Audrey tried not to believe that had been the reason, but the thought kept coming back, especially after it occurred to her that her father's serious condition could be why Beowulf had been insisting on spending so much time in John's bedroom lately. As if his doggy intuition was telling him he might not have much longer to be . . .

Audrey winced and tried to force herself to think of something else. But it wasn't easy. Sitting at her desk, she suddenly took a clean sheet out of her binder, spread it out, and got out the bronze pen. She stared at the pen and then at the empty page for a long time before she wrote anything.

Sometimes in the past it had seemed to work better if she wrote what might happen as part of a story. But this time what she wanted to say had nothing to do with any kind of fiction. This time what she needed the pen to do was just so completely nonfiction. At last she sighed, picked up the pen, and began to write.

I want my father to stop having angina pectoris.

She blew on the ink to be sure it was dry, started to fold the paper—and then stopped. Picking up the pen, she added another sentence to what she had written:

I want Mrs. Austin to stop being so mean to my mother.

Finishing the folding, she put the paper away in her secret novel binder and went to bed.

Audrey woke up the next morning feeling cautiously hopeful, but it wasn't long before her hope disappeared. At breakfast her mother was tense and quiet, and her father was, as far as Audrey could see, not any better. Cheerful and smiling as always, but not any less pale and shaky. His hands still shook when he picked up his cup, and his eyes, under his tilted eyebrows, were deep and dark rimmed. Audrey went on watching him out of the corner of her eye until he grinned at her, wiped his face with his napkin, and asked, "What's up, kiddo? Do I have egg on my face? You're staring."

Audrey was still denying that she'd been staring when the phone rang. Hoping to change the subject, she jumped up to take the call, even though she was pretty sure it wouldn't be for her. As usual, it was for her mother.

Hannah came back to the table looking puzzled and even more worried. "That was Dr. Richards," she said. She looked at John. "He asked if you could come in tomorrow at ten, instead of on Saturday." But when Audrey's father asked why, she only shook her head and said, "He didn't exactly say. Something about getting a second opinion."

When John asked if The Warden (meaning Mrs. Austin) would give her enough time off to drive him to the clinic on a workday, she nodded. "Yes," she said firmly. "She'd better."

It was just about then that the phone rang again, and this time it was for Audrey. "Who is it?" she asked her mother.

"It's Lizzie." Hannah looked puzzled as she handed the phone to Audrey. "I thought she was in Mexico."

"She is," Audrey said. And then, into the phone, "Lizzie? Where are you?"

"Hi," Lizzie's familiar voice said. "I'm here. Right back here in Greendale."

"But I thought—" Audrey was beginning when Lizzie said, "Yeah. So did I. But my dad found out he might get a promotion—if he was here next week. So he threw everyone in the van—at least everyone and everything he could squeeze in—and here we are. What a shock."

"Yeah, I guess so," Audrey said. "So you had to leave early? What a letdown!" What she was thinking was, *Hooray!* But what she said was, "When can you come over? Right away?"

"Well, maybe not right away. Hey, I got your letter and I can't wait to talk to you, but I have to help unload the van first, and believe me, that's going to take a while."

Audrey was frustrated. "Why do *you* have to do it? With all those brothers, you'd think—

"Yeah. You would, wouldn't you? But they've all managed to disappear. Must have hit the ground running."

Lizzie paused, and from a distance, Audrey could hear someone with a deep voice calling in Spanish.

"Okay, okay. I'm coming," Lizzie shouted, and then, quickly, "Bye, Audrey. See you. Sooner or later."

The phone went dead.

CHAPTER 24

AUDREY WAS STILL STARING AT THE phone when her father asked, "So, the Moraleses came home early? What happened?"

"Something about her father having to come back to get a promotion," Audrey said. "She sounded pretty frustrated. I guess she was really having a good time with some cousins." Audrey shrugged. "Too bad," she added, feeling a little guilty because she really wasn't a bit sorry. Not when there was so much she needed to talk to Lizzie about—the sooner the better.

Audrey's parents agreed it was too bad and went back to making plans for tomorrow and wondering about Dr. Richards's change of plans. Hannah sounded anxious, but John laughed and said it was probably because Doctor Rob wanted Saturday free to play golf.

It wasn't until Hannah left for work and John was busy with the morning paper that Audrey was able to spend a few minutes alone, making plans about what she would tell Lizzie and what might happen after that. But when Lizzie called again, a few hours later, it was to say that she wouldn't be able to come over until the next day.

"Not till tomorrow?" Audrey started to complain before it dawned on her that tomorrow might be best. For more reasons than one, it would be better for Lizzie to arrive while John and Hannah were at the doctor's. For one thing, if they knew Lizzie was arriving, it would mean that her parents wouldn't fuss at her to come with them. But even more importantly, there wouldn't be any witnesses to whatever experiments she and Lizzie might decide to do with the pen. Any experiments—like talking animals or baby dragons—that might be hard to keep secret in broad daylight.

Audrey went to bed that night looking forward to the next morning and Lizzie's visit, but the scene at the breakfast table was, once again, worrisome. John Abbott still didn't seem to be any better. And as for the other bronze pen experiment, the one about Mrs. Austin, nothing seemed to have changed there, either. At least when Audrey asked what Mrs. Austin had said when her mother asked for the morning off, Hannah only shook her head, frowned, and said grimly, "When I told her I had to have this morning off to take my husband to the doctor, she just turned around and walked away. Without saying anything."

Audrey's father grinned and said, "Well, it could have been worse. The Warden must have been in one of her better moods." And Audrey could only hope he was right, hope that the fact that the Austin woman hadn't yelled or said no might mean that one of her requests really was being answered. Crabby old Mrs. Austin was finally being a little nicer.

After her parents left, Audrey stayed on the front porch waiting for Lizzie, but not for long. It couldn't have been more than ten minutes until there she was, trudging up the road from the bus stop. Audrey ran to meet her.

They slapped hands and headed for the house, stopping only long enough for Lizzie to share a few welcoming bounces with Beowulf.

By the time they'd reached her room, Audrey had gotten around to saying it was too bad Lizzie's family had to come back early, but—. That was about as far as she got before Lizzie broke in: "*But* you've got news about the pen, haven't you? That's what your letter meant? That stuff about experiments?"

"Yes," Audrey said. "I wanted to tell you—"

"So did it do some new things?" Lizzie interrupted. "What did you find out?"

"Well." Audrey sighed. "Well, when I wrote to you, something had just happened that made me think it was still really working. That's why I wrote what I did."

She sighed again. "But before that I'd done two other experiments and nothing at all happened."

"Oh yeah? What kind of experiments?"

"I did two experiments about . . . well, about getting a new bathing suit."

Lizzie laughed. "You're kidding," she said. "You wasted a wish on a bathing suit?"

Audrey's face felt hot. "I know. It was a stupid thing to do, but it was just a test. And I guess it didn't prove anything. But then, night before last, I wrote two really important things. Wait, I'll show you." Getting out her secret notebook, she opened it to the page where she'd written:

I want my father to stop having angina pectoris.

"Good one," Lizzie said. "And . . . ?"

Audrey shook her head. "He's no better," she said. "Maybe even worse."

"And this one?" Lizzie said, pointing to where, on the same page, Audrey had written:

I want Mrs. Austin to stop being so mean to my mother.

"That didn't happen either," Audrey answered. "Yesterday when my mom asked her about taking the morning off, she just walked away without saying anything. I guess it could have been worse if she'd said no. But just walking away like that was pretty rude."

"Yeah, pretty rude," Lizzie said. She frowned. "But then, what was it that happened when it really worked? You know. When you wrote to me. Did Mowgli come to visit?"

"No." Audrey grinned. "I thought I'd save that until you got back. But what I did was to write some more of the detective story about the girl who could talk to animals. You remember that one."

"Sure, I remember," Lizzie said.

"I wanted to find out if I could get Beowulf and Sputnik to talk to me again. So I wrote this kind of afterword to finish up the story, and what happened then was the two of them talked, but just to each other, not to me."

Lizzie was frowning. "I don't get it," she said.

So Audrey turned to the page where she'd written the Afterword to "Heather's Alley Adventure," and after Lizzie read it, Audrey said, "See, I didn't realize that I hadn't mentioned anything about a human talking to an animal until the next day, but then as soon as I did, I could see that what I *had* written really did come true."

"I still don't get it. How'd you know they were talking if you couldn't understand them?"

So Audrey explained how she knew, going into a lot of detail about the way Beowulf and Sputnik had acted and the noises they'd made and how much better they'd been getting along since they'd had a chance to talk things over.

By the time she finished, Lizzie was grinning. "Yeah," she said. "Sounds good to me. You and that pen are really something. But I already knew that. Look at the way it got me home early. And"—she poked Audrey in the chest—"and look at my dad's promotion! The pen did that, too, I'll bet."

Audrey was bewildered. "Your dad's promotion? I didn't write anything about that. And I didn't say anything about you getting home early, either."

"Sure you did." Reaching in the pocket of her jeans, Lizzie pulled out a badly wrinkled letter and smoothed it out on the desk. "See right here at the end? Right here." Her finger was stabbing at the bottom of the page just above where Audrey had signed her name. Stabbing the words "See you soon."

Audrey gasped. "But that doesn't mean . . . I mean, I didn't say anything about you coming home early."

"No, of course not," Lizzie said. "You didn't have to. But soon is *soon*—not two whole weeks later. So the pen had to make it so I'd have to come back right away. So it got my dad the new job."

"Lizzie Morales," Audrey said, "I think you're crazy." But she was laughing as she said it. Laughing and hoping, or at least trying to hope, that Lizzie just might be right and that whatever she wrote, whether it was a story or just a wish, might come true.

CHAPTER 25

S O THERE IT WAS. THE BIG QUESTION: Did the pen really have anything to do with Lizzie's dad getting the promotion just so he, and all the rest of the Moraleses, would have to come home early, making Audrey's "See you soon" come true? Down deep Audrey couldn't quite believe it, but she really wanted to, for one reason in particular. And that reason was that if the pen had enough power to arrange Mr. Morales's promotion, that must mean that it was strong enough to answer Audrey's other requests. Particularly the most important one, about her dad not having angina pectoris anymore.

She told Lizzie so, and Lizzie said she thought that was one thing the pen would do for sure. "After all," Lizzie said, "that's the one that really matters. I'll bet the pen will do that one."

"But the other things that came true, like the one about talking to animals and the dragon thing, they happened right away," Audrey pointed out. "So how come my dad's not getting better already?"

But Lizzie had an answer for that, too. Well, sort of an answer, anyway. What she said was, "You know what? I think it must be that only really handy things happen right away. Like the talking to animals thing. Animals that were *right here* in your own house. That was quick and easy. But remember that 'See you soon' thing you did to me? That took a little longer. I had to get your letter, and then my dad had to find out about the promotion so we would have to hurry back. So maybe some things *are* happening right now, right this minute, that are going to make your dad better real soon. Maybe not today, but before long." Then Lizzie's eyes lit up like neon. "Hey, maybe that doctor is going to give him some new miracle medicine today, and in a few days he'll be good as new."

Audrey wanted so much to think so. To think that Lizzie's guess was a good one. Even just a little bit true. But when her parents came back from the doctor's around two o'clock, there was no sign of it. Looking exhausted, her father went right to bed, and as Hannah bustled around getting ready to go to work, she seemed and looked as tired and worried as ever. When Lizzie asked if she could ride back to town with her, she answered impatiently. "Yes, if you're all ready to go. I have to hurry."

Audrey tried to squeeze in a question about why Dr. Richards had made the extra appointment, but Hannah shrugged her off. "Nothing important," she said. "I guess he just wanted us to meet Marc, that nephew he's so proud of. He's going back to San Francisco tomorrow, and Doctor Rob wanted us to meet him before he left. Marc is a cardiologist. A heart specialist."

"A heart specialist?" Audrey said eagerly. "What did he say—about Dad?"

"Nothing much." Hannah sighed. "He seemed to agree with his uncle's diagnosis. You can ask your father about it when he wakes up."

She left then, taking Lizzie with her. As she went out the door, Lizzie put out her hand to be slapped and whispered, "Just wait. You'll see." Audrey stood on the front porch waving for several minutes before she went with Beowulf to sit on the floor in her father's room and wait for him to wake up. It took quite a while. Audrey was more than half asleep herself when her father finally woke up.

John Abbott laughed when he saw Audrey and Beowulf sprawled out on the floor next to his bed. "Nice pillow," he told Audrey. "As long as his stomach doesn't growl."

"No growls here," Audrey said, poking Beowulf's shaggy belly. "Just on this end"—she patted his big gentle head—"when he's in a dangerous mood." She got up and went to sit on the edge of her father's bed. "So," she said, "Mom said Dr. Richards's nephew is a heart specialist. Did he give you an examination?"

"Only a brief one," John said. "But he'd been over all of

Rob's records about my case. He did bring up the bypass surgery thing again, but Rob is still against it." He nodded thoughtfully for a minute before he went on. "I'd be willing to give it a try, but it would be very expensive and San Francisco is a long way off."

"Dad," Audrey said, "San Francisco isn't far at all if you fly."

"Well," her father said, "flying isn't exactly free either, and your mother would have to go with me and find a place to stay for a few days. And that would be expensive too." He put one arm around Audrey's shoulder and gave her a hug. "Don't worry, kiddo," he said, "I'll be all right. Nothing as boring as angina pectoris is going to get the best of an old newspaper man like me. I'll just write down 'angina pectoris,'"—he wrote in the air with one finger— "and edit it out." John Abbott scratched out what he'd written with his imaginary pen, and they both laughed, but Audrey's laugh didn't edit the catch in her throat.

She was still right there sitting on the edge of her father's bed when she heard a familiar but puzzling sound: the growl of a car's tires on the Abbotts' gravel driveway. It was only four o'clock. Much too early for her mother to be coming home from work. "I'll go see," she told her father. "I'll be right back."

When Audrey met her mother just as she reached the kitchen, she knew immediately that something was very wrong. Hannah Elgin Abbott's Homecoming queen's face was an ugly twist of pain and anger, wet with recent tears. Throwing not only her purse, but an armload of files and folders on the table, she sat down and buried her face in her arms.

Stunned into silence, Audrey stood without moving for several seconds before she put her hand on her mother's shoulder. "Mom?" she whispered. "What is it? What happened?"

For a while there was no answer, but finally her mother raised her head. "I've lost my job, Audrey. That woman fired me for taking the morning off," she said before she put her head back down and sobbed.

For several minutes Audrey tried to think of something to say or do, without much luck. She thought of saying it didn't matter, except she knew how much it did. Then she thought of saying something about Mrs. Austin, but the only words that came to mind were some that Sputnik used to say before he reformed.

Neither of them said anything more for quite a while. Then Hannah wiped the tears off her face and shook her head. "Don't tell your father."

"I won't," Audrey said. "But won't he have to know?"

Hannah nodded. "I'm afraid so." Her sigh turned into a shudder. "But the trip downtown this morning seemed especially hard on him. I'll tell him tomorrow if he seems stronger."

So they didn't tell him. Hannah explained her early

arrival by saying that someone else was taking her place for the whole day, which was more or less true. All the rest of the day Audrey worked hard on acting cheerful. So hard that, before the evening was over, her face felt stiffened by all the glued-on smiles. It wasn't easy, but it seemed to work. Her father seemed to believe their "everything is fine" act—or at least he pretended to.

It wasn't until after both her parents had gone to bed and Audrey had taken Beowulf on his bedtime outing that she felt free to go to her room. Instead of heading for his mattress in the living room, the big dog went on following her, following so closely that he stepped on her heels, right up until she sat down on the edge of her bed. He stopped then and stared into her eyes with his head cocked to one side before he licked her face, up the right side first and then the left.

He didn't talk this time, not really, but he didn't have to use words to tell Audrey that he knew she was hurting. And at that particular moment a sympathetic kiss, even a slobbery one, was all it took to break her up. Burying her face in the dog's shaggy neck, she began to cry. Beowulf waited patiently as she sobbed violently for several minutes and then a while longer as she shuddered with occasional sobs. Not until there was nothing left but a few sniffles did he pull away and collapse on his usual sleeping spot near the foot of her bed. It was then that Audrey got up and, wiping her face with both hands, went to her desk and got out the bronze pen.

Holding it in both hands, as she had done before when she was excitedly wondering about its magical power, she stared squint-eyed as she turned it from side to side. But this time, instead of excitement, what she was feeling was a painful, aching anger. Anger that it *had* granted her wish that Mrs. Austin would stop being so mean to her mother, but in such a terrible way. So now there would be no more of Mrs. Austin's meanness, but only because there was no more job.

It was like those old fairy tales where someone is given three wishes, and each wish is answered, but in ways that make each granted wish turn out to be a worse disaster. She could vaguely remember one about an old man who didn't really believe he'd been given three wishes and, when he sat down to dinner, carelessly wished they had some sausages to eat. And there they were, on the table. And then his wife got him to tell about the three wishes, and she was so mad at him for wasting one of the wishes on sausages that she wished they were hanging on the end of his nose. And so they were, permanently, until they had to use their last wish to get them off.

But Audrey's last wish—the most important one—was still out there—where there had been no answer at all, at least not yet. The angina pectoris was clearly worse, her father's heart was still hurting, and if there really was something that might make his heart well again, it was way out of reach. And what if her wish to have her father's angina pectoris stop would be answered by having his heart stop beating?

With the pen still clutched tightly in her hand, Audrey jumped to her feet and ran. Ran out of her room, down the hall, through the kitchen, out the back door, and into a moonless night, heavy with fog. A blinding blanket of mist that thickened as she climbed from one terrace to the next, until she was unable to see her running feet. But she kept going, stumbling and feeling her way until she got to the highest level. She stopped then, and turning to face the trail that went toward the cave, she held out the pen in both hands and whispered, "Why? Why?"

There was no answer.

She waited another long hopeless moment before she threw the pen as far as she could, out into the swirling fog. Afterward she wasn't at all sure whether she had only imagined a short sharp sound that echoed inside her head just as she threw the pen. A sound that might have been a shout or a squawk or perhaps a quack.

CHAPTER 26

THE NEXT MORNING AUDREY WOKE UP slowly, vaguely aware that it would be better to escape back into unconsciousness. But the comfort of drifting dreams refused to stay, and she was soon wide awake and, once again, filled with anger and anxiety. She was still trying, without much hope of succeeding, to sink back into forgetfulness when she became aware that somewhere in the house a phone was ringing. She looked at her watch—almost eight o'clock. She'd overslept. Still in her pajamas, she headed for the kitchen, where she found her mother talking on the phone.

"Yes. Yes. I understand," Hannah was saying. "And I do thank you so very much. Yes. Yes. I can be there by nine. I certainly can."

She hung up the phone, and turning to face Audrey, she said, "We have to hurry. It's late and I have to be at the office by nine o'clock."

Audrey was confused. "But I thought—," she was beginning when her mother interrupted.

"I know. I know," she said, and the way she was smiling told half the story. The half of it that let Audrey know it was going to have a happy ending.

"That was Mr. Macmillan just now." Hannah pointed to the phone. "You know, the district manager. And he said I'm to come back to work." She grabbed Audrey by the shoulders and danced her around in a circle. When the dance stopped, Hannah said, "And the best part is that Austin is leaving. They're transferring her to the Glenview office."

Audrey was stunned. "But why? I mean, how come?"

"I don't really know," her mother said. "Except that Mr. Macmillan said he was curious about why I'd been fired so abruptly, so he called some of the other people in the office." She almost giggled. "He didn't tell me exactly what they said, but I got the picture that some of them really stood up for me. And he wound up by saying that . . ." Lowering her voice and stroking an imaginary beard, pretending to be the important Mr. Macmillian, Hannah Elgin Abbott went on. "'I guess it just happens that way from time to time. Two capable and otherwise well-adjusted people for some reason just can't seem to work well with each other.'"

"Two well-adjusted people, my foot." Audrey snorted. "It's like Dad says. She was just jealous because you're so beautiful and she's such a—"Suddenly overtaken by a startling thought, Audrey asked, "Have you told Dad yet?"

"No." Hannah laughed. "No, I haven't told him anything. I thought I'd wait until after breakfast to tell him about being fired, and now . . ."

"And now you don't have to tell him about being unfired, unless you want to." Audrey giggled. She grabbed her mother's shoulders and tried to start another dance, but Hannah pulled her to a quick stop.

"I have to be there by nine. Can you get breakfast started while I change?"

Audrey could. And it wasn't until the table was set and she was getting out the cereal and milk that it suddenly hit her. Hit her so suddenly and so hard that she gasped and stood absolutely motionless for a minute with a box of cornflakes in one hand and a milk carton in the other.

The pen's power had answered her wish after all. And not in a cruel, sinister way, but in a good, helpful—only a little bit slow and roundabout—way. Just as Lizzie thought it did when it had arranged a promotion for her father so that Lizzie would see Audrey soon—sooner than she expected to.

Audrey got to her father's room just as Hannah, dressed now in her best work suit, was helping him into his wheelchair. Running into the room, Audrey quickly slowed to a stop. John Abbott's right hand was pressed against his chest, as it often was when the pain was bad, and his face was pale and clenched-looking. "Oh, hi," she said, trying to make her smile normal and ordinary. "I just wanted to tell you that breakfast is ready."

So there was a quick breakfast, Hannah left for work, and the day went on in an up-and-down way. Down, when Audrey would see the twitching muscle in her father's cheek that meant he was hurting, and then, a short time later, a little bit up, when his quiet smile showed that he was starting to feel a little better. The up-and-down times came and went most of the morning. And then in the early afternoon there was a phone call.

When the phone rang, Audrey thought it might be Lizzie, but an unfamiliar male voice asked for Mr. Abbott. Audrey took the phone to her father and waited.

John Abbott held the phone to his ear for a long time without saying much, and when he did begin to talk, he only said, "Well, that is very intriguing news, and I do thank you so much for your effort on my behalf." He paused and then went on. "I'll have to talk it over with my wife . . ." He smiled at Audrey and added, "With my family. Then I'll call back and let you know. Could you give me the number?"

He beckoned for Audrey to bring him paper and a pencil. Then he listened again and began to write, and watching him, Audrey somehow felt certain that what was happening, and what her father was writing, was very important.

"Who was that?" she demanded as soon as her father hung up the phone. "What did he want?"

John Abbott's grin was a little bit teasing. "Well, now. I've just received a piece of very interesting news. It's quite complicated, but good news, I think. However, it seems to me that we—you and I—should wait a bit to discuss it. Just until your mother gets home. It's the kind of thing that involves the whole family. A decision to be made that we'll all need to be in on."

Audrey begged a little, but it didn't do any good. Her father kept saying he thought it was something the three of them should discuss. But the way he looked when he said it made Audrey even more determined to find out. More and more determined as the hours went by. At one point she even thought briefly of having a temper tantrum, the way she sometimes did when she was a little kid and things didn't go the way she wanted them to.

Very briefly. She didn't know what having to deal with a temper tantrum might do to a person with angina pectoris, and she didn't want to find out. So she bit her lip and tried to find things to do to fill what seemed like endless hours until, at the end of the day, her mother's car came up the driveway.

And then there was another wait while Hannah Abbott finally came into the living room, smiling and full of news about how much better things were at Greendale Savings and Loan without a certain department head.

And John Abbott listened to her stories with maddening patience before he finally broke in and said, "Dr. Richards called today. No, not Rob, his nephew, Marc Richards."

"But I thought he left," Hannah said.

"Yes, he did. He called from San Francisco."

"He did? Why on earth would . . ."

Audrey clenched her teeth to stop herself from saying something like, *Just be quiet and we'll find out.*

"It seems," Audrey's father was finally able to say, "it seems that Dr. Marc Richards discovered that his hospital has recently been given a sort of grant. Some funds donated by a wealthy man who was treated, quite successfully it seems, for a heart problem very much like mine. So he gave the hospital some money that could be used to help pay for bypass operations for people who are good prospects for the surgery but don't have the means to pay for it." He grinned. "It's something you might call a 'bypass scholarship,' I guess. And he quoted a bunch of statistics that made it sound like the operation is becoming pretty routine."

"Oh, John. How wonderful." Audrey's mom's shining face looked almost the way it did in that old yearbook where she had been labeled the Girl with the Most Beautiful Eyes. She threw her arms around Audrey and pulled her down into a three way hug with her father.

"Hey, hey," John Abbott said. "Don't get too excited, now. There still will be the travel expenses to take care of and whether you can get the days off and—" But Hannah Abbott couldn't be discouraged.

"We'll do it," she said. "I know we will. I just know it."

Audrey felt the same way.

As soon as she could get away, she went outside, and in the evening dusk she began to search. Climbing from one terrace to another and back again, she looked under every bush and pawed through every patch of grass. But she didn't find the bronze pen.

CHAPTER 27

A UDREY'S NEXT FEW DAYS HAD A KIND of circular feeling, going around and around without really getting anywhere. Like a merry-go-round, or maybe more like a roller coaster. Exciting ups followed by depressing downs.

One of the ups was when Hannah's new boss said she could have a week off to go to San Francisco with John. And then came a down, when there wasn't enough money to pay for the airplane tickets or a place near the hospital where Hannah could stay.

At that point John started saying he thought they ought to forget about the whole thing, but Hannah wouldn't hear of it. Neither would Audrey.

But then things were up again when Dr. Marc Richards found a church near the hospital that had a room it loaned to people who needed a place to stay for a few days. And some of the people at the *Greendale Times* put John in touch with a support group for writers and editors, that came up with a loan that would cover some of the other expenses.

That left only one problem, but it was a big one. At least some people seemed to think it was. That was the problem of what to do about Audrey. Not to mention Beowulf and Sputnik.

Audrey didn't think that should be a problem at all. After all, she was the one who, for a long time now, had taken care of both Beowulf and Sputnik. And as for feeding herself, she knew how to make a lot of sand-wiches and a few other things. She said so over and over again, but nobody would listen. Nobody except Lizzie, that is.

Lizzie's solution was that she could move to the Abbotts for the week, to keep Audrey company and help with the chores. But neither the Abbotts nor the Moraleses liked the idea at all.

"What's the matter with parents?" Lizzie said on the phone after her mother and Audrey's mother decided not to accept Lizzie's offer. "They want us to learn to take care of ourselves and be independent, and then when you try to, they tell you to sit down and shut up."

And that was just the beginning. Lizzie had a lot more things to say the next day when she came to visit. Things like, "Okay. I get it. They just don't trust us. Oh, they don't say that, of course, but that's what it amounts to." She walked around Audrey's room, stomping her feet and throwing her arms around. "What do they think we're going to do the moment they take their eyes off us, I wonder? Start shoplifting or smoking pot? Turn into vampires?"

But a little later that same day, while Lizzie was there at the Abbotts', her mother called with another idea. One that Audrey's parents seemed to like a lot better. What she suggested this time was that her older daughter, Rita, who was nineteen, could stay with Audrey while her parents were away. Audrey wasn't too wild about the idea. It seemed a little too much like having a babysitter. And Lizzie was furious.

"She'll drive you nuts," she told Audrey. "Believe me, I know. We've shared a room all my life. At least, I get to share it if I don't ever wrinkle a pillow or drop a scrap of paper on the floor. Rita is a world-class neatnik. And she *hates* animals. Beowulf will drive her crazy, if she doesn't drive him crazy first."

But nobody listened to either Audrey or Lizzie, and that same night Rita moved into the Abbotts' guest room, and the next morning Audrey's parents left for San Francisco.

That first morning Lizzie's prediction about what living with Rita would be like seemed to be right on. Rita spent the morning cleaning house like crazy and looking like she'd just seen a man-eating tiger every time Beowulf got anywhere near her. And when Lizzie came over for lunch, she and Rita got into a big argument about who was going to do the dishes.

Then there was a phone call from Audrey's mom saying that they had arrived safely at the hospital and that John seemed to have made it through the flight and the ambulance ride to the hospital in pretty good shape. Audrey knew that old Dr. Richards had told her mother that he didn't think John was strong enough to stand the trip, so that was a real relief.

After she'd hung up the phone, Audrey couldn't help celebrating by twirling around a few times, and of course Beowulf joined in, bouncing around the room like an oversized jackrabbit. Lizzie joined in too, and the three of them bounced around the kitchen several times while Rita stood behind the table, clutching a dishtowel to her chest. But by that evening she seemed to be a little less panicky. At least she stopped trying to hide every time Beowulf looked in her direction.

The next morning Audrey's mom called to say that the doctors were doing a lot of tests and the operation wouldn't be until Wednesday. She sounded upbeat and cheerful, or else like someone who was trying to sound upbeat and cheerful.

On Wednesday, Audrey stayed near the phone most of the day, but wouldn't you know it, she and Beowulf had just gone out to the garden for a minute to pick some tomatoes when the call from Hannah finally came. So it was Rita who answered the phone, and when Audrey came in, Rita told her that her mother had called and said her father was still in intensive care but that he was doing as well as could be expected.

Audrey was disappointed—and worried. She'd been hoping to be able to talk to her father himself by then, and she didn't like the sound of "as well as could be expected." She plopped the tomatoes down on the table and went to her room to think. Of course Beowulf came too, and they sat down on the floor together. A few minutes later Rita came in.

"Look," Rita said, "I don't think you should worry. I'm sure everything is going fine." She went over to Audrey's bed, walking right past Beowulf's nose without even noticing, and sat down. "You know, I'm planning to go to medical school," she said, "and I've read a lot about different medical problems. It takes a while for everything to get working again after the kind of operation your dad just had. I'm sure he's doing just fine."

Audrey was relieved—and surprised. She certainly wouldn't have guessed that Rita was going to be a doctor. "Lizzie never told me," she said. "Does Lizzie know you're going to be a doctor?"

Rita shrugged. "I've told her so," she said. "But maybe she wasn't listening." She smiled. "I'm not blaming her. It's just that a lot of the time there's so much talk going on around our house that it's hard to hear what people are actually saying."

The next time Lizzie came over, Audrey told her about Rita wanting to be a doctor and Lizzie seemed surprised.

"I guess that explains it," Lizzie told Rita.

"Explains what?" Rita asked.

"Why you're such a neatnik," Lizzie said. "You know, like positively antiseptic."

That same afternoon Audrey showed Rita some of Lizzie's best caricatures, and Rita said she knew Lizzie liked to draw but she never realized how talented she was. "I guess that explains it," she said.

"Explains what?" Lizzie asked.

"Why you're such a slob." Rita was grinning. "I've heard that all great artists tend to be slobs."

That conversation happened on Friday, and it was the very next day when Audrey answered the phone and it was her dad. He sounded great. He said that they were going to fly home on Sunday and that he'd be back working at the *Greendale Times* before the summer was over.

And he was.

Also, by the time the summer was over, Audrey had started a new novel and two short stories, and she and Lizzie were working on another picture book for beginning readers. A picture book about an extraordinary white duck.

♦ ♦ ♦

Audrey went on looking for the bronze pen for a long time, but she never found it. However, she nearly always remembered to write wisely and to good purpose. And she never forgot that any furred or feathered creature could be an important messenger.